BLACK DAWN

By

James W. Bodden

First Montag Press E-Book and Paperback Original Edition November 2020

Montag Press ISBN: 978-1-940233-32-1
Design © 2020 Amit Dey

Montag Press Team:
Cover: Darkovo Je
Editor: Kathryn Sargeant
Managing Director: Charlie Franco

A Montag Press Book
www.montagpress.com
Montag Press
777 Morton Street, Unit B
San Francisco CA 94129 USA

Printed & Digitally Originated in the United States of America
10 9 8 7 6 5 4 3 2 1

DEDICATION

Para Orquídea, quien abrió mis ojos a los mundos escondidos dentro de las páginas de la colección de *Mil y Una Noches*. Los cuentos de "Los Siete Viajes de Simbad el Marino" y "Ali Baba y los Cuarenta Ladrones" fueron mis primeros pasos en el camino de la ficción.

Gracias.

TABLE OF CONTENTS

ACKNOWLEDGMENTS

I blame *Black Dawn* on Quentin Tarantino's *Kill Bill: Vol. 1 and* 2, George Miller's *Mad Max franchise,* and Kameron Hurley's *Bel Dame Apocrypha* series. These wonderful books and films deepened my fascination with street justice, antiheroes and the vigilante archetype, fighting for retribution against the backdrop of a world seemingly devoid of it.

Black Dawn wouldn't be possible without the hard work of Charlie Franco and the amazing editors of Montag Press who made this unforgiving world a reality. My special thanks goes to my indomitable beta readers Mario Rojas and C.F. Agurcia who stuck with me throughout this novella's many different iterations right up until the end of this journey.

CHAPTER ONE

THE PHANTOM

Scratched with static, the muezzin's call to prayer echoed across the desert.

Noor tracked the recording and bounded off-road, approaching a crumbling temple half submerged into the sand dunes. Its gates pried open with a boot to the lock. She shrouded herself and disappeared inside, keeping low and to the margins until she reached the bottom of the structure, a phantom balancing the divide between darkness and the light.

The temple's prayer hall was divided by a pair of honeycomb-patterned partitions. Noor pushed through the crowded chamber and slunk behind the screens separating the sexes for worship. Her kameez, leather slacks, and bandit's burnouse drew some curious looks from the widows and orphaned girls covered in traditional Drus mourning abayas.

She blew them a fleshy kiss, hid among the women behind the partition, and waited.

Then suddenly, all around her, Noor felt the ground shake. The foundations of the temple shifted with a powerful boom as the dome split apart and opened to the night sky. Noor's eyes met the dark sphere rising across the horizon, devouring the light of the stars.

"The Black Dawn..." she greeted the blackout shadowing the desert with a wink.

Soldiers burst into the prayer hall, dragging a band of war prisoners to the ceremonial altar, a blazing fire-pit fueled by a coil of gas pipelines. The men were chained, bound in death shrouds, and forced to kneel next to the flames. Night's eyes, jet-black obsidian stones, were stitched in place of their eyes to give sight to the dead on their final journey. The congregation went silent as the soldiers tossed the prisoners into the bonfire.

Noor watched the fire devour the bodies. She reached into her burnouse, pulling a pair of the Night's Eyes from the pockets. Noor flipped the stones in the air, seeking truths from a one-sided coin. But the talismans never answered. These false eyes were not for her.

"Sacrifice everything," Reza Pasha emerged from behind the altar, preaching to the crowd in the temple. "And she will give you one last chance to see the end of the world."

Pasha looked plump and soft, decked in expensive furs, but those dark veins gave him over easily. *No doubt about it,* Noor thought. This was the man she was looking for. Her first kill. Noor grinned, her lips as black as the night. *Time to get the action started.*

Noor kicked down the honey-comb partition with a loud crash, toppling it over and dispersing the entire congregation in a stampede for the gates, as she unsheathed the scimitar concealed under her burnouse—the curve of the steel reflected the altar's flames.

She peeled off her hood, dark veins spread over her bald head, "Missed me?"

"You're a dead woman," Pasha pulled away from Noor, recoiling from any forbidden intimacy between the sexes. "Nothing but a phantom from the other side."

"Other side? Hell's right here." Faith was the one habit she'd given up cold.

"What do you want?" he asked.

"Blood for blood."

Reza Pasha's eyes widened in dread as he watched her blade sweep through the air and chop one of his arms clean off at the elbow. His plump limb sizzled and spat in the fire.

At Pasha's scream, gunners spread out across the prayer hall and surrounded her. Four soldiers in plated armor closed in. Numbers were their advantage. Surprise was hers. She sprung the carbine rifle holstered to her hip and let it rip, mowing them down to a red pile by the pews. Her blood grew hot with the stink of nitrate, burned flesh, and gunsmoke.

Pasha drew a snub-nosed pistol from his furs and opened fire. He shot a clip of blind slugs, but only managed to wing her shoulder and earlobe as she dodged them. He was too slow; Pasha had gone soft. The rich life of an outback preacher had dulled his training and his instincts. That missing arm of his didn't help matters either. The warrior Noor had once known would never have wasted this many bullets on a close-quartered kill.

Noor flicked her scimitar and dotted Pasha in blood, "Is that all you've got?"

"You may not see them," Pasha lowered his voice; thick with fear, "but there are eyes watching us. If you kill me, you'll reveal yourself. Then, she will finally find you."

"That's the plan," she said. "I'm looking forward to killing the woman I love."

Hitting the striker on the hilt of her scimitar, she ignited a blaze of dark flames across the edge and swung, lopping off Pasha's head and sending it rolling to the ground.

Noor put out the flames, raised the saber to her lips, and blew on it like a hot spoon. She played the part of a devout mourner and walked circles around the prayer hall's altar, as the old rituals of the Drus religion required, then picked up the preacher's head, and shut his eyes before tossing him to burn with the rest of the carcasses crackling in the bonfire.

Spotting the gas pipes feeding the altar, she crouched down and patted the belly of the main line that led to the butane tanks buried beneath the ground. She cut into the pipe with her blade. A pressure leak whistled from the gash. Foul air screeched across the prayer hall as Noor doubled back to the top of the temple's stairwell and waited. When she could smell the stink of gas filling the chamber, she kicked up her carbine rifle and opened fire.

She busted out through the gates as the temple exploded behind her, fire scorching her robes. Hurled by the blast, her body rolled up and over the sand dunes like a rag doll. Concrete blocks, iron beams, and broken slabs of the dome scattered across the sand dunes.

A cloud of debris mushroomed into the sky as Noor limped out, the smoldering ruins of the temple behind her, pulling on the butt of a freshly lit, blue poppy-leaf cigarillo. Desecration of a temple was a grave crime for the faithful, but for an apostate on a rampage it was the spark to light a coming inferno. Noor was looking forward to meeting the woman she loved at the end of the world. Just the two of them. One last time before it was all over.

Noor cowled herself and bounded to the open road; she was just getting started.

CHAPTER TWO

TOMB WORLD

Starlight and the Black Dawn cycled one planetary rotation roughly every sixty hours on the planet of Nal Ghul, but with each turn on its orbit the blackout lasted longer and longer over the skyline. The sun was dying. Visibility dropped with each passing cycle. Only a faint spark flickered inside the core of the vanishing star. Darkness and the light were a dissonance of mirroring forces; one could only exist in the absence of the other.

Dead stars had never been encountered out in charted space. Talk of the phenomena was considered heresy, the height of foreign superstition, by the Drus religion. Monsters were not real, but nevertheless here it was and plain enough to see, the devil in the flesh.

Noor Malatesta lumbered down the broken-down road, bone tired, dragging her boots over the blacktop, her crackled eyes losing focus and blinking in and out of awareness. She stopped at the spine of a sharp hill, drank the last drops from her overheating re-hydrator, and scanned the desert outback with her night vision scope.

The road was open on all sides and left her vulnerable. No faction on either side of the war had the upper hand in the outback. Skirmishes broke out daily for control of the main road. She zoomed her scope on a mountain pass up ahead and decided to find shelter.

Darkness swallowed Noor whole as she moved through the gap in the mountain. A row of rock-cut crypts was carved into the heart of the limestone walls. Headless sentinels banded in hieroglyphs and tagged with graffiti rose from rubble piled inside the vaults. The mountain pass was a shrine to the Malak al-Maut, a long-extinct race of alien travelers. Native folklore was thick with their stories. Every tribe had its own legend about the gods that fell from the sky, but they all ended the same: death and darkness. These idols had stood watch over the desert for a millennia, but given time even immortals turned to dust.

Noor understood this better than most; she'd travelled the wastes long enough to see it for herself. Everything ends. No power could withstand the test of time. Every empire that bloomed from the rolling desert to the edge of the horizon was doomed from the start.

She steeled her nerve and ventured inside one of the crypts. Her boots crunched on a scree of rubble that echoed in the darkness. The vault was cold and silent and gave her the sense of a grave. A pang of anxiety got her heartbeat pumping again. She kept her guard up.

Noor approached a large head half-buried into the ground. The Malak al-Maut idol was massive, cracked into sections and banded in glyphs and pictograms spreading out like the branches of a tree. A sloping helm covered the alien's head but for its one, bulging eye. The decapitated statue's body loomed over her, its back supported the weight of the ceiling.

She slid down onto the idol's eye, hit the striker on her blade, and lit a poppy leaf cigarillo with the radiation-rich flames—a sparkling blue flare burned from the hemp paper's cherry. "Hell...," She groaned as the first wave of the opiates pulsed through her.

Keeping her hit short, she blew out the flames, and turned her saber to mirror her reflection. Her pale skin was sticky with sweat, gunpowder, and crusted blood. She looked like she'd taken a serious beating, her face blue, and black, and heavily scarred. The gaze of a happier woman hid behind a pair of hard eyes, but Noor could no longer recognize her.

A stink wafted from Noor's pits, and curdled her stomach. She reeked worse than the dead that she had left behind. Noor winced as she slipped out of her burnouse and kameez. The filthy linens stuck to the wound on her shoulder and tore the scab open. Blood dribbled down her body, the camber of her rib-cage, and the hungry curve of her hips.

She tore a strip from her kameez, wetted the rag with what was left in the re-hydrator and washed the blood to a pink slop. The rag slicked over a crescent-shaped arc of bullet holes scarring Noor from collarbone to navel. The marks puckered in the dim light. Noor ran her fingers over the scar tissue, like clockwork terrible ghost pains doubled her over to the ground. A salvo of bullets had torn through her and she relived the pain over and over again. Her memories were perfectly preserved, a wound that would never heal.

She gnashed her teeth and squeezed blood water from the rag over her head to keep herself together, washing away at the pain before it took her over and consumed her. Noor chewed on the butt of the cigarillo dangling from her lips. She pulled on the last of the smoke to take the edge off. Noor started to sweat as the blue poppy's signature hallucinations grew stronger and more vivid. Through her drugged-out eyes, she saw the sword in her hand melt away like a burning candle, dripping liquefied metal on her tongue.

Noor shook off the mirage and tossed the smoldering cigarillo over her shoulder. Hallucinations were never a good sign. She'd overindulged. Blue poppy leaf was a tricky habit to manage. It was a sweet but double-crossing lover. With every hit Noor took, she anticipated going too far, binging and teetering too close to the edge of an opiate overdose.

She curled into the pupil of the idol's eye and swaddled herself with her burnouse. The opiates made her sleep easier, but it was her saber that made her feel safe. She drifted off with her weapon wedged between her legs, thighs hugging the steel. Her thumb teased the striker, igniting a tiny eruption of black sparks as she fell into her own dark dreamland.

She couldn't manage more than a short nap. The sound of engines on the road roused her from her sleep. Noor rubbed the sand from her eyes and fished out her night-vision scope, focusing the lens on the lights of a large caravan. A convoy of transports and rigs were packed cheek to jowl, cordoning off a clutch of yurts. Sentries stood guard on top of freighter trucks, patrolling the camp with rifles slung over their shoulders. The Beiji nomad encampment bustled with carnie folk, pit fighters, contortionists, falconers, and leather-clad clowns gathered around the cook fires, drinking anise and moonshine, and roasting skewers of curried meats of lost and abandoned animals captured along the road. The women stuck mostly to their own, lingering by the yurts, and tending to their children and shaggy goats equally. A handsome minstrel plucked at a long-necked sitar for a crowd of onlookers, crooning a popular ballad for the vanishing, red sun.

"We're not alone...," Noor whispered to the idol's head.

She crouched behind a pile of rubble and watched Beiji dancers practice their routines in the camp. Young men swayed their hips, rung the bells looped around their bellies and shed long, colored veils to the ground. Scarab-carapace castanets marked their tempo and beat as the dancers moved seductively with the rhythm of the drums and fiddles.

The convoy's spotlights panned away from the dancers and targeted the entrance to the mountain pass. Noor scrambled backwards, blinded by the glare. Two sentries patrolling the camp fired warning shots and ventured into the crypts. Black, tightly-wound tagelmusts covered their faces, the mark of pit fighters, but their slim waists, lightness of step, and playful gaze gave them the look of perfumed dancers; all they needed were the veils and castanets.

One of the two Beiji tore off his tagelmust. The kid's mop of brown curls swept back with the wind. He lit the ground ahead with a lantern attached to the barrel of his rifle.

"Eyes open, Kamal," he said to the fighter beside him.

The Beiji's twin unmasked himself, peeling off the black rags from his face, and looked around, nervously, "It's the ghosts of the Malak al-Maut. They're watching us."

"There are no monsters, brother, only dangerous men," the pit fighter chambered a round; his slender body mirrored the shape of the bolt-action rifle. "Who's out there?"

"One of the monsters," Noor said, emerging from behind the stone idol's head.

"No more ghost stories," the pit fighter barked. "Get on your knees!"

"I'm not that easy..."

He raised his weapon, aiming dead between her eyes, "You could've fooled me."

"Listen close, kid, I'm a woman on bad business. Don't get in my way."

Kamal loomed behind his twin and whispered, "Maybe we should call for back up."

"Don't be a coward," the pit fighter said. "She's a just a junky on her last overdose." He moved closer, his lantern lit the black veins sprawled across her skull. "She's too ugly for the pimps at the oasis, but the salt mines always pay well for chattel."

"Not one more step," she warned. "Turn back, forget all about me, drink yourself to sleep, and wake up in a pretty Beiji dancer's bed, but don't make me reach for my blade."

He dared her with his next step, "You'll be dead before you touch the hilt."

The walls of the crypt closed in. Noor was cornered, an animal working on instinct alone. She fought the drive to violence, but had never been any good at taming the monster inside. Noor drew her scimitar in a single fluid slash, ripping the pit fighter's throat open. The Beiji pit fighter dropped to his knees, desperately trying to hold back the blood flowing through his hands. He reached out and called his brother's name without making a sound.

Noor turned to the other twin, "You look smarter than your brother. Drop the gun!"

Kamal nodded and put down his rifle, spitting out a Beiji curse under his breath. He cradled his brother into his arms, hugging him close, pleading with him to stay with him.

The kid's blood dribbled down Noor's cheeks. She wiped the red into a streak and backed away from them, shaking her head. A knot squeezed in the pit of her stomach. No matter how hard she tried or how fast she ran away from herself, death always followed.

"I warned him to stay out of my way," she muttered more to herself than Kamal.

"Help me. He's dying."

"I'm sorry, kid, but he's already dead."

"You're lying," Kamal cried.

"Let me teach you a first lesson," she said as she snatched a canteen from the dead Beiji. "Only death pays for justice in this tomb world. When you're ready, I'll be waiting."

Gunshots fired from the road. Noor clocked a new band of Beiji pit fighters rushing toward the alien crypts. She moved quickly, aimed her carbine at the decapitated statue holding up the ceiling and tore it to pieces with a strafe of bullets, raising a cloud of heavy debris as the vault came crumbling down, covering her escape from the mountain pass.

Back on the road, the dying star rose over the outback and shadowed after Noor. A cold shudder swept through her and it wasn't the temperature dropping. Guilt slowly ate away at her.

When she was far enough to be alone, she went down on one knee and swallowed a scream that had buried itself inside her like her blade into the kid's throat. She punched the asphalt, peeling the skin off her knuckles. But it didn't help, one pain didn't faze the other. Noor knew the rules of the game. Many more innocents would suffer so she could finally get her revenge. She would balance the scales of fortune one death at a time.

She looked over her shoulder and zoomed her scope into the outback. The Beiji scouting party hunting her down had disappeared into the desert, but she wasn't alone. Far out in the sand dunes, she spotted Kamal crawling on his belly and stalking behind her; he was hiding behind a large sarsen, rifle was aimed on her, but too far away for a clear shot.

Noor turned around, giving him a big, easy target, every step like walking a plank.

CHAPTER THREE

FAULT LINE CITY

Noor stabbed her blade into the sand and zeroed her scope on the canyon breaking across the desert; the display read two-point-one klicks, and detected no hostiles in the area. The wreckage of an enormous dreadnought, embedded into the walls of the canyon, spanned the entire width of the gorge like a bridge. This place was the end of the road, the last stop for desperados, deserters, and would-be exiles. Travelers called it Fault Line City.

A fleet of ships lifted off from the dreadnought and glided across the sky, making the jump into low orbit. Noor's mind wandered every time she watched the transports fly away. Nahl Gul's elite paid a fortune to buy themselves passage off this dying rock. The rest of the 'unclean' masses were left behind to war over the ashes and witness the end of the world: the moment the planet froze over, its atmosphere dissolved, and an endless night swallowed every last star in the heavens. Noor had always dreamed of escaping the desert, rocketing into space, and losing herself in some dark corner of the galaxy; but these reveries no longer drove her, she'd given herself over to more vital desires: vengeance and blood. Noor flicked off the fleeing ships and gunned it for the gates of Fault Line City.

Rows of tents and metalwork shanties split the hull of the massive dreadnought into a grid of winding roads and alleyways. Drus colonists from across the great wastes travelled in reptile-pulled trains, lorries, and wheeled rigs; their women, ragged and veiled against the weather, were penned on separate, flatbed speeders that rode at the tail-end of the lurching convoys. Entire settler populations, uprooted and displaced to rove the world over in an endless migration, searched for the last traces of heat left on the planet. Traffic surged and crawled to a halt, but never stopped here. Fault Line City was the only waystation bound for the equator. Its concourses were always packed, a shifting blur of movement illuminated by the artificial light from the inbound and outbound transports.

A muezzin's call to prayer cut through the roar of traffic. Noor followed a congregation of natives, brindled jackals and Qabila tribesmen gathered around a monk preaching to the faithful over a bonfire. The Qabila were cloaked in flowing white robes draped over lithe but powerful frames. Linens, bound around their legs and feet, showed sharp talons through gaps in the fabric. The jackals knuckle-walked on all fours like low animals, their bodies covered in matted fur. Like hundreds of off-world species across the galaxy, most of Nahl Gul's natives were converts to the Drus star fire religion, the faith of the eternal flame that claimed to bind every world and lifeform in this universe together.

"Fools...," she muttered through clenched teeth, "...there's never just one."

Noor cowled herself and mixed in with the faithful. She mouthed the prayers with them, but never dared say the words out loud for fear that somehow, if said just right, this ritual would take her over. Sometimes, in her weaker moments, Noor still craved the balance in her heart that came with her old connection with the stars' fire. She was an apostate now, a *kafir*. She'd walked away from her religion, and all religions, with eyes wide open.

Noor leaned on a lamppost by the sidewalk. The roads overflowed with traffic. Starlight faded from the sky and darkness approached. Noor's clock was ticking and picking up speed. "I don't have time for this nonsense," she muttered, throwing herself into the incoming traffic. Rigs and speeders honked and hit the brakes on the road, crashing into a pileup. Traffic surged all around her as she leapt into the air, desperate to find a way out of this mess.

She shot over the swerving ships and landed with a flip on top of the roof of a rig. The craft veered between lanes, scraped into a speeder with the impact, and screeched its wheels as it hurtled away on the tarmac. She piggybacked on the rig for a few more blocks until the transport reached the gates of the flesh markets. Noor jumped overboard at the curb. The scar-tattooed gangbangers at the gates circled, flipping stiletto-thin daggers at her, gesturing in their pantomime until she paid their toll and slipped through the gates.

War veterans staggered out of the taverns and cheap roadside brothels. Panhandlers huffed downers through mechanized respirators and begged on every street corner. A couple of drunk recruits shot themselves over a whore up ahead, while

Noor slunk into an alley packed with johns on queue for the rent boy bent over the drains. She shot the soldiers a dirty look as they buckled down for their turns, tossing coins into a pile on the ground.

On the other side of the alley, Noor strolled past a group of pilots for hire chugging down starshine and playing games with three round dice. She scanned the pilots over, but they were a pitiful congregation of old men and shell-shocked alcoholics. Noor approached a helmeted veteran slumped over a bottle, the only one of the whole lot that wasn't knee-buckling drunk, and booted his rum straight into the gutters on the other side the alleyway.

"Can you fly straight?" she growled.

The man went for the sawed-off shooters holstered on his hips; he raised the barrels, sizing her up through the sights, "Trust me, no honest captain promises a straight route."

"You don't look that honest to me."

The captain lowered the shooters and dropped his helmet into his lap. Jet on red, geometric runes tattooed over his black skin. "Seth Cain," he saluted. "Janissary Core. Retired."

"Nice tats, captain," she said, looking him over.

"A popular fad among veterans. Earned by body count."

"Is your bird ready to fly?"

"All I need is a destination."

Noor looked over her shoulder, "The front."

"I run girls to the capital all the time," he pulled down her hood, exposing a web of black spider-veins, "but you're not the type they're looking for. I can tell you that for sure."

"No," She cocked her hip and exposed the hilt of her scimitar. "I'm not."

"I only take hard currency on this dying planet, no credits." The captain stretched out his palm. "You know how it goes. The end of the world brings out the worst in us all."

"Every single one," Noor agreed, tossing him a burlap bag chockful of copper coins. "I'm in a hurry. We must take advantage of the darkness and head on out with the dawn."

Cain struggled upright on a bionic prosthetic leg, moving slow and deliberate. "Then we must hurry," he said, shuffling the coins in his hand as he counted them twice. "The night's almost over."

Noor followed the captain through the rows of tightly packed ships stationed on the tarmac's outbound concourses. Cain's cruiser was stationed on the hangars at the stern-end of the hull. Unfortunately, though her bet on a pilot was now sealed, the ship was a scrap-metal rescue, dented and refurbished with mismatched wings. The captain's old jalopy looked like it would disassemble apart in midair, if it managed to hold together at liftoff.

Noor shook her bald head. "This bird is going to drop like a stone."

"Trust me," Cain said. "She's not pretty, but she knows how to ride."

The captain limped into the cruiser to fire it up for takeoff. The engines throttled, sputtered off, and then reengaged. Thrusters burned and lifted the swaying ship from the runway. Noor took a stroll around the tarmac while the ship's engines warmed up. Piles of refuse burned at the edges of the concourse. Orphaned urchins scavenged the trash with prosthetic claws, bagging metals to trade at the city's foundries and smelting factories. Her vision tunneled in on a Beiji stalking low through the piles of trash, the kid's face covered in a tight, black tagelmust. Kamal's lean body cast a blade-thin shadow across the ground. His rifle was pointed at her. She grinned, blowing him a kiss across the billows of smoke.

Suddenly, a sonic boom reverberated across the concourse. Noor freed her saber from its scabbard out of instinct, the steel gleamed with the stars. Her drugged-out eyes went wide on the cataphract gunships flying across the sky, closing in on Fault-line City.

"The Fallen...," she snarled, recognizing the dark Fedayeen's signature war ships.

The cataphracts hovered over the concourse like vultures. Hooded riders saddled the open cockpits with boots planted on the wingspan. The gunships nosedived. Their rotary cannons opened fire with a hissing screech and all hell broke loose. A salvo of bullets cratered and ricocheted off the tarmac. Fuel drums exploded. The crowds surged in panic. Scavengers pitched off the hull. The generators blew and a blackout spread across the dreadnought. Noor was surrounded, outmanned, and outgunned smack-dab in the middle of the Fallen's kill zone.

One of the Fallen jumped ship and landed on the tarmac. Dark, chitinous armor glinted from underneath her robes. A familiar gaze was visible through the warrior's turbaned-helmet. Wild green eyes glared at Noor from below a cruciform visor. Noor's grip tightened on her blade. She recognized the woman under the great helm, Sadira Rah.

"You look like you have one foot already in the grave," Sadira's voice scratched across the tarmac. "Maybe you should've stayed dead. Nobody plays a corpse like you..."

"I've never been good at just lying around," Noor shrugged.

"I'm not complaining. There's no greater thrill than watching you die."

"Let's settle scores then. Blood for blood. Mine for your false god's."

Sadira Rah shook her head, pity in her gaze, "You'll never lay eyes on her again." She drew her scimitar in a swipe, connecting with Noor's blade. The weapons crashed together, held under tension for a drawn out second, and broke apart with a scatter of sparks. The blow sent Noor reeling across the tarmac. She rolled to the edge of the dreadnought, but managed to break her fall before the drop, her boot catching the lip. Noor hauled herself back on the concourse, heart pounding, with a sudden itch for a hit of poppy.

The lights of an incoming ship blinded Noor. She went for her carbine and braced for an attack, but the cruiser swooped in and blocked Noor from Sadira Rah's path. A pair of machine guns dropped from its wings and strafed the Fallen's gunships. The riders, taken by surprise, pulled back from their positions and sped away in different directions. Seth Cain gave Noor a playful wink from the cockpit and mouthed the words, "Take-off."

Smoke and burning fuel thickened the air. Transports roared as they sped away from the concourse and scattered. Noor got up and ran for the cruiser's blast doors, but the Beiji emerged from the crowd and blocked her path. The kid's rifle pointed at her bald head.

Slipping under his barrel, Noor decked the kid with the hilt of her saber and dropped him inside the ship's cargo hold. She jumped in after him, slamming the pressurized hatch shut. Her body fell backwards, banging her head against the deck as the blast doors bolted and locked. She crawled on all fours over to the cockpit, "What are you waiting for? Fly!"

"In three, two, one," Cain engaged the cruiser's thrusters and lifted off, jumping past the packed take-off queue. Turbulence shook the craft as it rocketed off into the sky.

"I didn't think this bird of yours would make it off the tarmac," Noor slipped into the passenger seat next to him, muck-caked boots propped up on the ship's control panel.

"You can trust me," Cain punched the accelerator. "Question is, can I trust you?"

"No," she answered, pressing her face to the porthole to watch the lights of Fault Line City fade as the ship gained altitude, leaving the great gap splitting the desert behind.

CHAPTER FOUR

BLOOD FOR BLOOD

The ship broke out of sub-orbital flight and made a hard descent back to the desert. Noor Malatesta stormed into the ship's commode as the landing gear hit the rough ground. She doubled over the squat-toilet and retched bile. The bowl flushed with brackish water. Her back up against the wall, Noor couldn't stop her body from shaking. Her pale skin was slick with a cold sweat while she burned with a fever. Noor lit a cigarillo to shake off the pangs of the withdrawal sickness. The soothing opiate pumped through her bloodstream with the beat of her heart. Noor hung her head back, casting a long shadow on the toilet.

She heard footsteps in the corridor and busted out of the commode, meeting the captain by the cruiser's pressurized doors, holding the cuffed Beiji pit fighter at gunpoint.

"You look like the dead," Kamal snickered.

"Getting there," she croaked, and then turned to the captain. "Why did we stop?"

"There's a skirmish up ahead on the comm band. Easier to wait the bastards out than to go around them, and we certainly can't go through them in the middle of a fight."

"I needed some fresh air anyway," Noor said, jumping out of the pressurized hatch.

The cruiser had landed on top of a flat mesa overlooking the desert. Cain built a fire pit by the bow-end and began his dawn prayers, counting down his prayer beads, and tracking the dark star's ascent into the sky. He finished his prayers and blessed himself to complete the ritual, rubbed his hands in the rough earth, and narrowed his eyes on Noor. The captain and his client glared back at each other across the fire. Trust was running low.

Cain took a swig of starshine off his flask. The vanishing light outlined the close crop of his raven hair. Noor recognized the faded shield of the Caliphate's elite Janissary core on the captain's pauldrons. The daredevils of that select squadron were skilled pilots. If this was indeed Cain's armor and not something he picked off a corpse or a pawn shop back in the dreadnought shanties, everything was available for a price on a dying planet.

"What do you want to do with the boy?" he asked. "I say gut him."

"Let him go."

"Are you crazy? First chance this desert rat gets he'll shoot us in the back."

"The risk's half of the fun," she smiled, wolfishly.

The kid squirmed against his restraints, curls spilling over his face. He blew away a coil of hair, "I got no beef with a veteran. But this killer owes me and I'm here to collect!"

"You'll try," Noor drew her saber and slashed the steel down on the kid.

The Beiji's restraints cut loose. The kid shuffled the cuffs off and backed away from the fire pit. Kamal swept his yellow eyes from Noor to the captain and then back again.

Explosions blossomed across the skyline and lit up the mesa summit. The blitz thundered and rolled over a set of distant ruins rising from the borders of the outback.

"Lights in the sky mean a slaughter," Noor said as she bit down on a cigarillo.

"We're getting close," Cain said, "to the War for the End of the World."

"Not close enough..."

"Are you a believer?" The captain met her eyes. "Do you think we'll win the war?"

"Not a chance," she snorted.

"Our enemies are few, but the mullahs' armies are the many. It's been foreseen: the Fedayeen will destroy the Fallen, take back the star temple, and bring our sun back to life."

"Men are either fools or fanatics. I don't believe in lost causes."

Seth Cain stood from the fire pit; his dented armor shifted as he straightened into a stiff, military posture. His face looked sweaty and was beginning to paunch with the drink.

"Back in Fault Line City," he focused his icy gaze on Noor, "I'd never seen the Fallen hunt after one of their own kind before. You are one of them, aren't you? A Fedayeen warrior who turned her back on the one, true religion to worship the devil."

"Leave it alone. Don't ask a question if you don't have the balls for the answer."

"Well, I'm not flying closer to the front until you tell me what we're doing here."

Noor's teeth gnashed with the taste of metal in her mouth; her words came out slow and bitter, "I'm on a killing spree. A real bad one. And you don't want to get in my way."

"Something doesn't square," Cain closed the gap to Noor, bionic leg dragging behind him, and pointed a finger to her face. "Tell me, what are you really fighting for?"

Noor drained her cigarillo to a nub and flicked the butt over her shoulder. She wriggled her body out of her burnouse and lifted the threadbare kameez underneath, exposing the bullet holes scarred into the flesh of her chest and her belly to the pit fire.

"Blood for blood; and I'm talking gallons," Noor snarled. "My beloved Khadija and I were the first Fedayeen to fall. The first to see the sun go black. She was the light of my life, but she was taken from me by the Night Mother. Now, I mean to get her back, murdering every one of the Fallen that gunned me down and tried to stop me the last time."

"What will you do when you find the woman you love?"

"Burn her. My blade's got one purpose, captain. Revenge."

It grew quiet around the fire pit as the barrage in the sky intensified. Cluster munitions detonated on the borders of the desert, bombing the ancient ruins and monoliths. The Beiji broke the silence. He slowly leaned into the fire pit; his eyes dilated with fear.

"Do you know what the Night Mother is?" he asked. "Have you heard the stories?"

Noor chuckled. She liked this kid despite him hating her guts and wanting her dead and buried. Women like her didn't have the luxury of friends, only enemies or accomplices.

She puffed out a slither of smoke, "All right, kid; tell us a good one."

"Every tribe from the poles to the cataracts tells the same story," he said by way of protestation. "The Malak al-Maut have risen from the grave and walk the world again."

The Beiji shook as he told his story. Kamal was short but lean, with outsized gunner's hands that didn't fit the line of his frame. The kid wrapped a band of black cloth around his face, covering his lips, pyramid jawline, and bronzed skin. He tightened the fabric into neat coils, shaping a perfect tagelmust with a narrow slit across his eyes.

"The stories are true. All of them. The Beiji masters sat around the camp fires and told us about the old legends, but no one listened. Nobody believed. They said that the Malak al-Maut would reveal themselves again on the night the red sun died out. The Night Mother has risen to awaken her sleeping children and cast a Black Dawn over the world."

Noor closed in on Kamal, smiled, and blew a cloud of poppy smoke into his face. "Don't worry about her, kid. Everything ends. Even an alien playing at god can be killed."

"What man can slay an immortal?" he sneered. "The Malak al-Maut have finally returned to take back this planet. The Beiji masters say nothing will stop them this time."

She put out the cigarillo underfoot, "The trick to killing a god is not believing in it."

"What if I can't help but believe?"

"Then you're already doomed," Noor shrugged.

She wandered away to the lip of the rocky mesa and watched the explosions ripping across the sky. The fallout reflected off her eyes, lighting the fires burning within her. The captain lumbered to her side and took a belt from his flask, pointing to the battle to the east.

"The skirmish is almost over. The skies will clear up. What's next?"

"Ready the ship, captain," Noor croaked. "I want to go for a dip at the oasis."

CHAPTER FIVE

THE HANGED MAN

A gale of wind shifted her mantilla of veils. The woman hiked her mourning robes, dragging the hems like a serpent's tail across rows of freshly dug graves; along each one, shields were buried at the foot of the dead as tombstones. From there, she wandered to the foot of a hangman's tree at the heart of the boneyard. The oak's gnarled branches were heavy with hundreds of rotting corpses suspended from ropes and chains. Steel cages swung overhead; inside, skeletons cooked into their chainmail clung to the bars.

The shadows of the straggling oak vanished as the Black Dawn crested over the sky. She pushed back her mantilla and let a mop of blonde curls tumble down the small of her back. Her pale skin drank in the light of the stars like a hungry stone. She circled around the tree and spotted a man, hot blooded and alive, looking down from one of the cages.

A thief, roguish and black-bearded, met her gaze. His voice was weak but eager, tinged with seduction. "The Black Dawn isn't safe for a woman on the road. You're just asking for a tragedy."

Her milky eyes fixed on his, "I'm a mother of dead children. Tragedy is all I know."

"I can help you survive," the thief gripped the bars, "if you set me free."

"What makes you think I'm afraid of the darkness?" the Mother asked.

"You should be. My tribesmen are riding from the cataracts to get me out of this cage. These are brutal men. If you help me, I can save you the worst of their savagery."

"Is that why they put you inside that cage, for your savagery?"

"The soldiers that dug this mass grave are the real savages," he said. "I was only trying to make a living. Scavenging bodies is easy money. Who can resist easy money?"

"The trouble of stealing from the dead is that it takes you closer to the grave."

"Don't worry about me," the hanged man smiled. "Death and I got ourselves a deal. We walk hand in hand, but we don't touch. It's a convenient arrangement. She gets a real man and I live. Death's a lovely lady once you get to know her. I'm one lucky devil."

"You must be quite the catch to tempt a god."

"Unfortunately," the young grave robber pointed at a gang on horseback approaching the mass grave through the bars of his cage, "you'll never find out."

The bandits rolled in kicking up a cloud of dust and earth. Two masked gunners trained their rifles on the woman under the tree, circling around her. A pack of hairy jackals were chained to the horses and knuckle-walked behind them. One of the gunners pumped his rifle and shot down the branch holding the hanged man's cage; the pen dropped to the ground with a loud crash, rolled over to the graves, and busted open.

The thief jumped out of the cage and sauntered toward her, cackling with the riders holding the chains on the pack of jackals, "I warned you. The Black Dawn's not safe."

"But this is where I belong," the Mother said, "among the dead and the dying. I am on a pilgrimage to spread the great revelation of the galaxy, the paradise of the night."

"Beautiful and crazy," he laughed, nodding at the tribesmen who dropped a coil of rope on the ground. "You can only end in tragedy. Let me keep you safe until nightfall."

She cracked a half-smile, "I'm not the one who's in danger here. That black star in the sky is dying. The end is near. You must witness the great revelation before it's too late."

"I'm not looking to join some new-fangled Samarak cult," he snickered.

"You will see the truth the moment you die."

"I told you, me and my lady death have ourselves a deal. I'm going to live forever."

She glared her milky, white eyes on him. "You are no god."

"Only in the sack," he grinned.

"You say you know Death." The Mother's mourning veils swept back as the wind picked up with an incoming sand storm, revealing the plated pistols holstered at her hips. "But you can't recognize her when she's finally come for you."

She drew the pistols and opened fire. Both gunner's heads burst open, a splatter of brains and shattered bones. She turned on the jackals charging at her and shot them up into a bloody pile. The spooked horses reared up and dropped the corpses off their backs.

A trail of smoke billowed from the Mother's pistols and banded across her white eyes. She closed in on the young man, barrels aimed for a close-ranged, grisly head shot.

The thief backtracked, stumbling on the graves, "Mercy, momma..."

"I can offer you something better, lift the veil from your eyes, and let you see."

"What do you want to show me?" his voice cracked.

"The end...," she whispered. "You have two choices: close your eyes, or stare into the void. The void will stare back and reveal its great mystery. The paradise of the night."

"I'm afraid..." the grave robber blessed himself.

"Only because you were blind," the Night Mother raised her pistols and fired, drilling two scorched bullet holes into the thief's eye sockets, "but now you can see."

The Black Dawn climbed to its summit, covering the entire outback in darkness. With every passing cycle, the sun dimmed and slid closer and closer to the other side, and she could not wait to watch it collapse into pieces and tear apart like old bones. Shadowing over the rows of graves, the Mother jumped on the back of one of the rider's mounts, a pale mare that was nothing but rib bones, and galloped into the desert to preach her revelation.

CHAPTER SIX

THE SIREN'S STRIP

Dropping dead-stick, the cruiser shut down its main thrusters and circled around the outskirts of the waterfront outpost on the other side of the desert: the Oasis of Ulaan-Rum.

Noor popped the exit hatch and jumped out onto the ship's wingspan. Her body rocked with the shifts in drag and turbulence as she teetered over the cuff of the turbines.

"Coming in nice and quiet," she said to no one. "Never let them see you coming."

Cain nodded from the cockpit as he reengaged the engines and leveled the ship behind a rock formation across from the Oasis, giving Noor enough cover to go unnoticed.

Disembarking, Noor flipped through the air, knees hugged against her ribcage, wind cutting at her skin. The mad rush from the drop kept her pulse racing and haywire. She landed in a crouch, the folds of her burnouse wafting out around her like a blur of smoke.

Down the road, a crowd of fatigue-clad soldiers lined up by the oasis' docks, waiting for the ferries travelling the nighttime waters to take them across. When she got there, Noor pushed through the throng of stinking sex tourists, boarded the next boat, tossed the rusted droid pilot a couple of coppers, and took a seat on the stern, just over the rudders.

Mirrored solar sails rose as the ferry raised anchor. Noor put her boots up on the lip of the gunwale, leaned back, and relaxed for the first time in a long while, enjoying the loll of the ride. An armada of sailing ships, trireme boats, and pleasure barges glided over the water. The Oasis of Ulaan-Rum was the only live spring in a thousand mile radius, but its clear waters were beginning to darken, toxify with methane and ammonia, and slowly freeze over. Nothing was meant to survive without the healing light of the sun. The mirage of bygone, idle days evaporated under the sights of the war ships anchored on the far side. Noor could see the slow panning of the railguns, tracking targets moving in the distance.

As she sat there, backsplash from the other ferries sprayed a slosh of ice on the deck and soaked Noor over, much to the pleasure of the passengers who took this trip often. Shivering, she jumped up from her seat and shook the wet off like some wild animal. Along the approaching coast, rising from the waterfront, a row of lavish palazzos lined the boardwalk of the Siren's Strip, the red light district's infamous brothels and casinos.

Noor jumped off the bow the moment the ferry docked on the pier. She shouldered past the hawkers peddling skewered goat meat, and rushed toward the lights of the strip. The thoroughfare was packed with a slow-moving crowd slipping in and out of the many brothels, teahouses, and high-rise casinos. Low-res holograms flickered over the pavement, their naked dancers streaked with static, inviting tourists inside the competing palazzos, the forecourts of which were mayhem. A procession of sword jugglers, hooting clowns, and fire-breathing buskers swirled around Noor, but the main show was up on the balconies where the oiled bodies of the sirens glistened in the night. From below, Noor watched the whores dance, snaking their torsos near the rails. The desert-raided girls and choice-dancing boys from the Hamada stripped off their kimonos to tease the growing crowds on the streets. The prostitutes' faces were hidden behind masks molded in the likeness of the Malak al-Maut. Discount sirens on the lower balconies wore cheap masks forged out of copper, the expensive whores in the middle sections were decked in silver headdresses, and the concubines on the upper penthouse levels gleamed with golden, alien battle-helms.

The Oasis of Ulaan-Rum was a haven for pleasure, luxury, and indulgence--if you could afford them. Its sirens were the most famous seducers and spies on this planet. Further along the street, turbaned pimps in grizzly furs sat on a corner cafe, sipping mint tea, and sharing poppy from the tentacles of a narguile. Half-naked girls, chained to their masters, snuggled on the hairy men's laps, hand-feeding them from bowls full of sugared dates, sand crab dumplings, and peppery cardamom seeds. At the far side of the street, Noor jumped the curb, hand hovering over her scimitar, ready to slice them open if they gave her any trouble. As she walked past, she shot the pimps a disgusted, sidelong glare.

"Flesh dealers..." she spat on the ground.

Noor brushed past the pimps on the street cafe, and climbed the steps to the large palazzo, gleaming in white stone, on the same corner of the strip. Inside the vestibule, she sniffed out the glass, egg-shaped elevators, and rode them up to the penthouse suites, a mere shadow to the concierges and procurers. On the top floor, she slipped out and walked through a hallway painted over in a tableau of frescoes that depicted the sun rising over Nahl Gul's great deserts, its famous Devil's Range in the distance. The corridor rounded the top floor until it reached a dead end and a pair of double doors. Knowing exactly where she was, Noor's boots did the knocking and broke the lock as she stepped inside the room.

Ismet's slender body leaned over the bed like bait. Her silken, embroidered kimono draped over the curve of her hips, thighs, and scaled tail. The golden mask of a scarab covered her face, and revealed a sliver of her nocturnal, reptilian eyes. The alien giggled.

"You're late," the siren said, removing the mask. Ismet's green scales were banded in tattoos and false eyes. Her undulating tail reached out and tugged at Noor's burnouse.

Noor spotted an open bottle of starshine by the bedside. She smiled, took a healthy swig, and paced around the room; she was an animal testing out the limits of her enclosure.

"You got what I want?" she asked.

"I'm a siren of the oasis," Ismet said. "I can sate any desire under the Black Dawn."

Ismet slipped off her kimono from shoulders to hips to the ground, the silk coiled at her bound, deformed feet. She pressed her naked body against Noor's and pushed her on the bed; straddling her hips, grinding slow and building up heat. The lovers' breathing turned thick, thighs wetting as their bodies pressed harder against each other, and the friction between them mounted. Noor slipped her hands under Ismet's panties and raked her nails into the base of the reptile's tail. The siren slitted her forked tongue and moaned.

Noor grabbed the siren tight, pressed her chest against hers, and saw the face of her beloved looking back at her. Khadija's lips parted open. Sweat dribbled down pale skin. Yellow curls covered her eyes. Noor kissed her, but felt nothing but scales and fangs.

In a panic, Noor pulled away from the siren and pulled herself together. The blue poppy hallucinations were hitting her faster and harder, lately. She had to lay off the drugs.

"Enough with the games," she said.

"What...," Ismet covered her fangs and giggled, "no foreplay this time?"

Noor gripped the siren by the throat, blowing her a fleshy kiss, "Next time."

"There are no second chances in this world," the siren hissed. "What do you want?"

"Only what I am owed," Noor slipped her free hand between the siren's legs and found her sex. "I didn't pay for your skills under the sheets. What I want's information."

"Lucky for you I deal in both," Ismet groaned, softly.

"I gave you a list with five names on it. Reza Pasha. Joh Mustafa. Sistani Amin. Sadira Rah. And Khadija Al Barakat. Your job was to find them while I take them out."

"I gave you Pasha," she said, clutching her thighs. "The Fallen are tricky to find."

Noor closed in and wrapped both hands around Ismet's neck, "The Fallen gunned me down and left for me dead. Stopped me from stabbing the woman I loved in the back. So you see, I'm eager to get on with my rampage. Payback's been a long time coming."

"You were once a Fedayeen warrior, but you have forsaken them, then you turned on the Fallen and the woman you loved. What side are you on? How can I ever trust you?"

"You can't," Noor shrugged, "Betrayal comes too easy for me."

"I should never have agreed to this. You bring nothing but death with you."

"I won't ask again," She squeezed harder. "Where are they?"

"You always play so rough?"

"Always..."

"I got what you want," Ismet winked, "but it's going to cost you."

"Fine...but if your information's a dud I'm coming back for you."

Ismet pulled Noor's hands from her neck, "Let's start with Sistani Amin. The general leads the Night Mother's armies in the capitol and holds the line at the front. Sadira Rah is roving the outback, hunting after you; but I suspect you already know that by now. This other woman you are looking for, Khadija, there is no trace of her. She's a ghost."

"What about Joh Mustafa?" Noor asked.

The reptile darted its forked tongue, "He's right here."

"Where?"

"Look for yourself," Ismet sauntered across the room and opened the drapes to the balcony, flooding the room with the crackling street lights. "Joh's closer than you think."

Noor stepped onto the balcony. She drew her scope and zoomed-in on the penthouse on the other side of the boardwalk. Behind the terrace's glass doors, Joh Mustafa laid on a hot brothel bed, rolling around with two expensive prostitutes wearing golden battle helms.

A twisted grin crawled up Noor's cheeks as she unsheathed her scimitar.

She turned to Ismet and tossed her a scattering of copper coins. The alien dropped to her knees and scooped up the loose coins in the hems of her kimono.

Noor tightened the grip on her saber. The thrill of the hunt only grew with every kill for her. This scared Noor more than anything. She could feel that she was starting to get off on violence, finding pleasure through the pain of those that had betrayed her. *I am heaven's sword,* she repeated a verse from the holy book of the Drus. *Justice in the guise of death.*

CHAPTER SEVEN

ONLY DEATH PAYS FOR JUSTICE

Noor made a run for the balcony and leapt over the rails, flipping across the span of the boardwalk and crashing through the terrace into Joh Mustafa's penthouse suite. Dark flames burned across her saber as she levelled the fiery weapon at her old friend's head. The sirens screamed and darted from the bed, knocking over a charcoal brazier on the rugs and animal hides piled on the floors. A smoking fire spread in a flash. Joh Mustafa chuckled and dragged himself out from under the bedsheets. He stood with the fire rising at his back. Sweat slicked the web of black veins sprawling on his thick-set, muscular body.

Noor remembered Joe Mustafa as a deadly Fedayeen warrior, strong, quick, and always popular with the ladies. None of his talents had faded by binding to the dying sun. She would have to be careful. Joh was known to cut men in half with a swing of his blade.

"Noor Malatesta," Joh Mustafa dragged his massive scimitar across the ground, sparks ignited with the friction. "I heard a ghost story that you were back from the dead."

"Tell me, was it a scary one?" she asked, taking a step closer.

"Only for you." Mustafa puffed his chest. "Are you here to finish what we started?"

"You always could read my mind." She smiled.

Noor whirled her saber and smashed into Mustafa's weapon, but the Fallen deflected the strike and countered with a riposte, cutting a gash down her sword arm. Studying his careful, deliberate moves, she danced around him, trying to find an opening. As Mustafa came back at her, Noor found one and sidestepped him, slashing a matching wound on his black-veined bicep. Drawing first blood made her go hungry for more violence. She swung her blade, recklessly, but Mustafa blocked it, and knock her down with a knee to the gut. The Fallen Fedayeen raised his scimitar for a decapitation strike.

She got up, unsteadily, shielded behind her saber. "Do it!"

Mustafa dropped his scimitar like a hammer on Noor's blade. He pushed his weight on the crossed blades and inched them towards his opponent's head. The pressure dropped Noor to one knee, then both. Panic hit. Her heartbeat pounded. Hot adrenaline surged through her bloodstream, pumping her full of the primal drive to claw, bite, and rend to stay alive. This might be more that she'd bargained for. Mustafa was stronger, sober, and a better swordsman, but Noor had always intended to play dirty for this kill. She hit her saber's striker and summoned a ripple of dark flames. The fires burning across the penthouse rose up the walls, radiation rising as the flames flipped from red to black. As if answering her cry, the dark inferno converged around them, devouring Joh Mustafa whole.

Noor's eyes went wild and alive as he burned. She pounced on his smoking body, drilling her scimitar into his chest with a downturned, icepick grip. Mustafa's ribs cracked with a red spray. Noor straddled his hips as the flames went out, and pushed the steel in deeper. He died bleeding between her thighs. Noor wailed her fists on his charcoaled face. Knuckles peeled back raw with every punch. She couldn't stop herself. Mustafa's skull soon collapsed and became unrecognizable. Noor dropped on him from pure exhaustion, laughing like a crazy woman. She climbed off the corpse, stumbling and gasping for breath.

Noor lit a cigarillo and pulled out to the terrace to make her getaway. She slipped out through the curtains, but got sucker-punched by a steel gauntlet, and knocked back into the penthouse. Noor's vision blanked out with the punch on the side of her bald head and only slowly came back into focus as she began to recognize the woman standing over her.

The Fallen's chitinous battle-armor gleamed with the embers of the fire as she closed in on Noor and nicked a scimitar under her throat—blood smeared the steel's edge.

"I knew you couldn't resist coming in for another kill," Sadira Rah's voice scratched under her helm. The deadliest of the Fallen. Not even Noor could compete.

"How did you find me?" Noor asked.

"You're not the only one paying Ismet," Sadira said. "Whores are easy to buy."

She looked back at the charred body on the floor, "So Mustafa was just bait?"

"He was handsome, but ordinary. You on the other hand, are uniquely dangerous."

"I am...," Noor peeled her ragged kameez and bared the arc of bullet scars branded into her skin. "You and your killers shot me twelve times, but I've come back for more."

"You were the first Fedayeen to follow the Night Mother's path, bind with the dead star, and gain its power. But you were also the first to betray her and stab her in the back."

"I followed Khadija because I loved her," Noor said. "Not to start the end of days."

"You never deserved her."

"You loved Khadija once too. But she picked me. Get over it."

"She's not who you remember," Sadira said. "You don't know what she's become."

Noor chuckled. "Khadija is just another mad woman that thinks herself a god."

"Are you ready to kill the woman you love?"

Noor peeled her scimitar from its scabbard. "I don't make the rules of the game, Sadira. She took everything from me. Only death pays for justice in this tomb world."

"You poor fool. If you're looking for justice you came to the wrong place for it." Sadira Rah hit the striker on her blade, opened its vents, and sparked a ripple of dark fire.

Noor hurled herself at her, but Sadira expertly deflected the blow, swatting her away with a slam that sent her crashing to the penthouse's balcony. Sadira followed Noor outside and drove the scimitar through her gut. Steel plucked out with a trail of smoke.

"Can you feel the pull of the Black Dawn?" the Fallen asked. "Its shadows have spread over the entire world to hunt you down. The Night Mother is calling for you."

Noor crawled backwards against the railing. A red streak trailed behind her and puddled over the tiles. Her saber went out. She looked over the edge to the oasis below.

"I am not afraid of her..." She muttered, the words mostly for herself.

Sadira Rah lifted her cruciform visor; only her wild green eyes, the broken ridge of her nose, and a hint of her black lips showed through the chitinous suit of battle armor.

"Then you will die," she snickered.

Noor flicked Sadira off and blasted the woman back with a shot from her carbine rifle. She smiled, jumping over the rails into the waters below. Her body dropped like a stone. She dunked in the oasis with a heavy splash and sunk into the freezing deep. Noor pushed herself to the surface, breaking through the ice. She swam for the docks and made it to solid ground, coughing out rime, and gasping for air. The docks looked empty. The crowds were gone. No ships moored on the pier. Out on the road, headlights blazed down on her. Two cataphract gunships sped straight for her from opposite ends of the dockyard.

Noor pressed her palm on the wet wound and dashed into the darkness of the desert.

CHAPTER EIGHT

BOGEYS

The gunships kicked up a whirl of smoke and strafed Noor down across the desert, bullets ricocheting and debris fragging all around her. Noor's boots flattened the spent ammo casings as she gunned it away from the Fallen that were closing in, hot on her trail.

She hurtled herself down a steep sand dune, broke hard on the ground below, and turned her scimitar on the incoming gunships, a crooked grin crawling up her face. Beneath her, the earth shook. Sand dunes crumbled apart, the terrain shifted, and the earth displaced over the ground in a landslide. The captain's cruiser emerged from underground and flew up into the sky. Finding her spot perfectly, Noor rose with it, straddling the spine of the ship. She waved at the cataphracts as they rocketed off and flew after her in pursuit.

Noor dropped into the cruiser's cargo hold and collapsed just outside the cockpit. Her teeth were red, dripping blood, and gnashed like some wild predator from the outback.

"We got bogeys on our tail," she cried out.

"I see everything," the captain hollered from inside the cockpit.

A blinking, blue signal glowed from the cruiser's dashboard. The captain tightened his grip on the wheel, and made a hard turn right. Thrusters screamed with the shift in direction. Cain elbowed the Beiji sitting next to him. "Is she dead or alive back there?"

Kamal rolled his eyes, and jumped out of the cockpit to check on her. She looked pale and bloody and wouldn't stop shivering. The kid poked her with the toe of his shoe.

"How can you tell the difference?" he sniggered. "She always looks half dead."

Noor rolled over and coughed out a wad of blood. "You're funny..." she croaked.

She tried to get up, but the turbulence knocked her back on the deck. This time she stayed down and crawled over to the portholes on the stern-end of the ship. Her knees buckled as she struggled to look through the panes. She left a red handprint smeared on the glass. Outside, Noor spotted three cataphracts moving fast and closing the distance between them. Fallen Fedayeen were piloting the vehicles and maneuvering into a triangular attack formation from where they opened fire. Noor hit the deck as bullets tore through the side of the cruiser. The ship rocked with the impact. A fiery column of fuel flared up from the fuselage. Cain gripped the wheel and gradually managed to stabilize. He turned from the cockpit and shouted at Noor, "Damn it, woman! How'd you get the Fallen so riled up?"

"We're just old friends." She tried to laugh but the pain in her gut was unbearable.

"Pardon me if I don't buy it," Cain said. "How about we give them a show?"

The captain helmeted himself and braced behind the wheel. He punched it, accelerating the cruiser, veering towards a monstrous sandstorm blowing in from the south. Turbulence rocked the flying jalopy as it maneuvered through maelstrom, veering wildly from port to starboard, trying to lose the gunships riding close behind them safe in their slipstream. The cruiser boosted its thrusters and climbed higher and higher into the upper reaches of the atmosphere. Noor fell backwards, knocking her bald head on the deck. The sudden shift tossed Kamal across the cargo hold, crashing through the commode doors. The cruiser careened into the clouds. Its engines overheated and the thrusters started to smoke as the fuselage rocked like it was about to blow apart in midair.

"This bird's going to drop!" Noor barked at Cain, crawling into the cockpit. She jumped on the seat next to the captain and searched everywhere for the buckles and straps of the safety belt, but the ship had none – not that it surprised her one bit.

"That's the plan," he said, calmly. "In three, two, one..."

With a sudden gravitational shift, the captain killed the engines and let the cruiser drop. The ship lost altitude, and in doing so gained momentum. Red lights glowed on the dashboard and an alarm screeched as the rust bucket nosedived into the sand storm below them. Cain reengaged the thrusters and accelerated, speeding straight for the ground.

The gunships, having followed them straight up, altered course and dove in after them, battered by the sand, getting closer and closer to their slipstream. They were close.

Seth Cain winked. The cruiser's afterburners engaged at max power and the ship pulled up to the sky again, flew upside down over the gunships in a loop, and came in to fire at their rear. With one hand on the steering controls, the captain expertly manned the machine guns on the wings, blasting the cataphracts to pieces across the desert outback.

Counting in his head, "one more to go," Cain swept his eyes across the storm. "Where is she?" the captain screamed out, unable to lock in on the weak signal on the dash.

Noor pointed to the porthole, her eyes widening.

"Behind us!"

A lone gunship, too far behind the pack, had tucked in behind their loop-de-loop move and now its sights were locked on the cruiser. The rider's hood swept back to reveal a cruciform helm. Sadira Rah reared the engines and opened cannon fire against her enemy.

Noor gripped the secondary launcher on the passenger's seat, manning the heavy parallel machine guns under the wings. Spinning her barrels to aim behind them, her eyes zeroed in on the dash's crosshairs. An alarm blasted as the target locked on the sights. She licked her lips and let the gun rip. A streak of lights exploded in the sky. The blitz of crossfire blinded her, but she wouldn't let go of the launcher or the trigger. She hooted like a jackal, shooting in a rage until her gun cashed out of ammo and locked. The skies were silent for a moment. Noor slammed her fist into the dashboard, and snarled, 'Fuck..."

Sadira Rah's gunship was still there. As it shrieked back into range and trailed after the cruiser, it fired a direct hit on their thrusters. The cruiser's engines exploded with a thundering boom. Fire rose over the hull as the ship spiraled out of control and nosedived.

CHAPTER NINE

THE CATACOMBS

A sandstorm blurred out the desert horizon. Noor pushed against the gale, leaving the fiery wreckage of the cruiser behind her. She shrouded herself against the dull sting of the dustup and drifted, blind and losing her sense of direction, haunting the fringes of the outback like a phantom. But being lost had never fazed Noor. The trick was always to keep on moving. Never stop. She'd wandered through this planet for all of her life and knew that sooner or later even the great wastes came to an end, as long as she could survive that long.

Through a break in the storm, Noor spotted the captain and the Beiji half a klick out; the men were climbing a formation of rugged steps carved out of a sheer sandstone cliff. She followed after them and approached the strange architecture of stairs, battlements, archways, and catacombs that tunneled into the hollow of the mountain ahead. There, she struggled up the rock-cut steps, bleeding out a red trail on the ground, her sight losing focus. She couldn't shake the pain anymore. Soon her body went cold and turned unresponsive. Vertigo swept her over as the fear hit. She lost her balance and collapsed. Falling, Noor tumbled down the steps of the cliff and blacked out when she hit the ground.

* * *

Darkness lifted, slowly. Her vision was blurred. All Noor could make out was that she was shivering on the floor of some dark cave in the network catacombs and tunnels that burrowed deep into the bedrock of the mountain. The sandstorm raged and howled outside. A pale, red glow bathed over Noor's body. She turned her head and gauged her surroundings. The walls were carved with rows upon rows of fire-lit vaults, keeping a collection of stone heads buried inside. The idols were sculpted in the image of the Malak al-Maut, aliens carved in the likeness of crowned sphynxes, basilisks and battle-helmed djinn; a terrifying grotesquerie from the bestiaries of the galaxy looked down on her.

The pressure of a barrel on Noor's head made her turn back. She traced the length of the rifle and met Kamal's eyes through the sights. Noor chuckled, wincing from the pain.

"What do you want, kid?" she groaned. "Can't you see I'm busy dying here?"

"Is it true? Are you one of the Fallen?" Kamal asked.

"That's right," Noor nodded. "Guilty as charged."

"I've never met a dark star fire binder before... I thought you weren't real."

"Oh, we're real." She snapped her fingers and lit a spark of dark fire that quickly snuffed out. "Fedayeen use the sun as the source of their power, but we bind to dead stars."

"You have seen it then... the Night Mother?" his grip shook on his weapon.

"We've met," she pressed her palm on her bleeding wound. "Be a good kid and grant a dying woman her last wish; light me some poppy before I pass out from the pain."

"That flesh wound won't kill you," Kamal pumped the fore-stock of his rifle. "I will. You're going to pay for everything that you've done. Starting with my only brother's life!"

"Believe me, kid, I haven't forgotten anything I owe you..."

She gripped the barrel and jerked the rifle aside. A sudden shot went off. The barrel heated up and singed her palms as she savored the pleasure of the burn. In the second that she had while he watched, mesmerized, Noor swept her boots out, heel first, and kicked the Beiji's knees in. She jumped on the kid, tore away his rifle, and turned the barrel on him. A crooked grin crawled up her face. Everything moved too quickly. Her body was still weak. Her fever spiked. Noor was too sick and nowhere near battle honed. She wasn't ready for a fight, not that a fever had ever stopped her before. Her blood dripped over Kamal's chest.

"You can't kill me, kid. Not yet, anyway."

Kamal shrank back against the wall of the cave. His curls veiled over his face and its growing bruise. He looked younger than he really was. He blinked, eyes slick with tears.

"I was never any good at fighting," Kamal said after a long while.

"The masters told me I wouldn't last my first season in the pits. But my brother promised me that the old men were wrong; he said I would live if only to spite to them. And he kept his promise to me. Mahmoud saved my life more times than I can count."

He paused.

"But I couldn't save him once." Kamal's face lined with rage. "You're the one who taught me that only death pays for justice in this tomb world. All I want is my revenge!"

She looked into his eyes and recognized a familiar darkness growing behind them. The kid's rage mirrored back someone she knew well. The reflection she saw was her own.

Noor threw his weapon back at him. "Let me teach you a second lesson, wait before you strike. Watch your enemies close, learn, let their guard drop, and then kill them all."

"I'm no good at waiting..."

"Believe me, I know the feeling well," Noor held out her hand to him. "But fair is fair, kid. When I'm done with my rampage you can start with your own. I won't fight you."

Kamal recoiled from her and didn't shake it, "Why should I trust a killer?"

"You shouldn't," she answered, closing her open hand into a fist.

Kamal strapped his rifle on his back and wiped his cheeks. He walked around the chamber staring at the strange stone heads watching from the walls. "What are these?"

"Fetishes," Noor said. "The Hashara bugs still worship the Malak al-Maut."

The Beiji shuddered. "I hate bugs."

"A long time ago, before the caliphate colonized Nal Ghul, the Hashara queens ruled over a great empire. The bugs' subterranean hives covered the entire outback."

"What happened to them?"

"We did." Noor shrugged. "The Fedayeen razed the bugs' fortresses, tore down their cities, smashed their idols, and drove the species into warrens deeper underground."

Cain limped into the cave; his prosthetic leg dragged behind him. His shooters were out, chambers loaded with buckshot. He swept the gun from Noor to Kamal and back again.

"I heard shots," he said.

"Just a bit of friendly fire," Noor shrugged.

Cain turned to the Beiji. "Is that right?"

"We were just playing around." The kid rolled his eyes.

"The storm's fizzling out," Cain said. "We have to keep moving."

"Not yet," Noor pointed to the mouth of the cave. "They're still out there. The Fallen won't stop until they hunt me down, and they'll kill anything that gets in their way."

Cain holstered his guns, "Then we need to lay low and go underground. The bugs' catacombs cut right through this desert. I know someone who can offer us sanctuary on the other side of the tunnels. But I warn you, Noor, we're in hostile territory. Bug country."

The captain collected his flask, ammo, and the other salvageables he'd managed to rescue from the wreckage and bounded off toward the catacombs; having nowhere else to go, and no one else to trust, the Beiji followed him into the maze of underground warrens.

Noor lingered behind, bleeding from her belly. The glowing fetishes in the walls gave her skin a jaundiced hue. To quell the pain, she smoked a poppy leaf cigarillo, pulled out her Night's Eyes from her robes, and flipped the obsidian stones, seeking truths from a same-sided coin. Noor always kept the stones close - one last talisman of her old religion. She kept them safe for a worthier person than herself, somebody that deserved saving.

Noor had seduced Khadija into smoking poppy. Both of them would wait out the dawn, burning opiates on top of the Star Fire Temple's cupola, sparring with their blades and making love at the foot of the great bonfire lighting the summit of the structure. But Khadija never took to addictions the same way Noor did. She always knew when to stop and had saved Noor countless times before from an overdose. From the first day they had met, soon after both girls had been culled from their families and taken to the great temple, Khadija had never left Noor's side. That day they found each other in the crowd and held hands. They had been together, one way or another, from that moment. But, unfortunately, good times never last. Khadija had become something Noor could no longer recognize.

Holding in the smoke, Noor swept her saber in front of her. She knew she had to keep on moving, but she wasn't ready. Noor had to heal herself first and she needed to find the courage to do it. She chomped on the cigarillo some more to get back her lost nerve.

"I'm not looking forward to this." She exhaled a puff of smoke. The effects of the drug hit her hard. She was already high and as ready as she'd ever be. It was now or never.

Noor gripped her scimitar and hit the striker—the steel came alight and glowed with the heat. She shifted the blade into a *seppuku* suicide grip, aimed at her own bowels, and pressed the steel onto her flesh, cauterizing the wound shut. The pain was unbearable. Noor's scream boomed across the Hashara catacombs and woke the stone heads buried into the walls. The idols opened their thousand eyes and watched her disappear into the tunnels.

CHAPTER TEN

BUG COUNTRY

Noor's boots sunk into the earth with every step. The waft of bug stink thickened the air. Sprawling outgrowths of lichen and fungi glowed on the ceiling and lit the mounds of salt stacked up in rows. Deep in the catacombs the vast mines unfolded through the underground for miles. Piles of smooth, rounded stones were arranged into cairns in every tunnel of the bug's network. Noor wandered the mines, scanning the area with her scope.

"We took a wrong turn," she muttered. "What the hell is this place?"

The captain unholstered his shooters. "This is bug country."

Noor scanned her scope again. The Hashara were unpredictable and territorial animals. The bugs took no mercy on interlopers passing through their lands – not after everything that had happened to them during the caliphate's colonization efforts. The hives had sided with the Night Mother and the Fallen in the War for the End of the World, inciting a bloody insurgency to reclaim their ancestral territory from the foreign invaders.

The captain picked up his pace and moved on out. Kamal trailed behind them; the kid was busy kicking the stone cairns and toppling them over. For one brief moment, Noor thought she saw the rocks move on their own and stack themselves back together again. She rubbed the grit off her eyes and tried to ignore the blue poppy leaf's hallucinations. A few feet away, Noor spotted something snaking low on the ground. The creature winded closer and closer to her, twisting between the mounds of salt and the piles of smooth cairns.

"We got trouble," Noor croaked.

The bug's mechanical exoskeleton rose up on its spindly legs. Its milky body writhed inside a piloting pod. The crawler pressed against the porthole, screeching. It was a female, a bug alpha; the Hashara species' only sentient gender. The pod's mechanized legs grinded and reared into the air, kicking up the earth and salt beneath it. The bug alpha raised itself to meet Noor and Cain's eye level, and warbled at them in its mother tongue.

"Easy, girl," The captain bowed to the creature. "How's the health of the hive?"

The crawler's pink eyes seethed from inside the pod. Wet, albino folds wriggled as it smashed against the porthole and splayed its mechanical legs in an aggressive stance. Seth Cain translated the creature's language, coolly; he didn't show a hint of emotion.

"We're trespassing on her hive's land, it says."

"What does it want?" Noor studied the bug alpha.

The captain raised his pistols in front of him. "Revenge – on us."

A twister of salt and sand spun into the air as the crawler lunged, its exoskeleton's pistons and gears grinding as it closed in. A bladed tail sliced through the air and speared at Noor. She dropped to the ground and ducked out of the way of the incoming blade. The crawler shook and screamed in its screeching tongue, cursing at missing its target. Noor backed up from the alpha, but had to stop when she felt movement behind her. She looked over her shoulder. The cairns stacked around the saltpan started to stir. Every pile toppled over and a nest of insects scuttled on the ground. The sentry males of the hive, who were watching and hiding under the cairns, swarmed. Noor's eyes widened as the hive closed in.

"Scarabs!" she screamed.

The captain swept his pistols and opened fire. Bugs exploded to pieces in midair. Gore splattered on the ground as feed for the rest of the cannibal hive. A big, calico-backed scarab jumped off a salt heap and lunged at Noor's neck. It snapped its mandibles, but she snatched the pincers away before they bit and ripped them apart in her bare hands. The bug dropped and she stomped it into sludge under her boots. Screeching boomed from the other side of the tunnel. Noor turned with her saber leveled at mid-range. She went cold as the bug alpha slashed its bladed tail. Thinking fast, Noor sidestepped the weapon. The tail gored inches from her face. She gripped her own steel, hit the striker, and ignited the scimitar. Waiting until the alpha was within reach, she swung the blade and melted through the crawler's mechanical legs. The bug shrieked and tipped over in a scramble of earth and gravel. A pressurized hatch popped on the belly of the piloting pod and the bug wriggled out of the wreck, tunneling into the earth towards the safety of its underground warren.

Noor spat on the earth, marking her territory over the bug alpha and her hive. She beat her chest and cackled like a crazy woman. Dust kicked up behind her. She turned around and spotted Kamal down on the ground, rolling, kicking, and screaming, fighting off three big scarabs crawling all over him and chomping at his limbs. Noor ran up to him and held the Beiji down to stop him from squirming and making things worse; the deeper the bugs were able to dig in, the closer their mandibles came to snapping his bones apart.

"Scream all you want," she said to him. "This is going to hurt like hell."

She tore the insects off his flesh, and tossed them over her shoulder. The scarabs hissed, flew up into the air, and barreled back at her. And just as she raised her steel to meet them, the insects burst into slush all over her face. From behind them, Cain was shooting the bugs down. The captain emptied his barrels until he pushed back the rest of the swarm.

"Pull back!" he shouted.

Noor dragged the wounded Beiji out of the tunnels and Cain guarded their rear as the bug's screeching echoed behind them, retreating to the surface and out of bug country.

CHAPTER ELEVEN

WE ARE THE MONSTER WE SEEK

Noor stood on a remote bluff in the desert, shrouded under the folds of her indigo burnouse. She balanced on the lip of the rock, bone-tired, swaying with the wind currents. Noor wanted desperately to give in to her exhaustion. Only fear kept her body going.

She swept her night vision scope across the horizon and kept a lookout for signs of any incoming gunships. Her paranoia was keyed up, raised to a hair trigger. Every little thing that moved across the outback set her reaching down for her fire sword in a panic.

Suddenly, lights sparked in the distance. Noor spotted the bogey coming in from the skies of the north. Her crew armed themselves and braced behind the rocks for incoming gunfire as the craft veered towards them, but the ship turned out to be a freighter on route over their position. They all laid down their weapons, rifle, shooters, and scimitar. After a long silence, the Beiji went off by himself to the bottom of the bluff. He plopped down on the sands below them, and sparked some poppy he'd swiped from Noor when he thought she was deep asleep. But Noor didn't sleep anymore. Not since this rampage started. She let the Beiji keep the drugs, even though the desert rat deserved to be taught a lesson; but she was in no mood to play at being a mother. She had more vital concerns to deal with tonight.

"If the Fallen find us...," Noor couldn't finish the sentence on her own.

So the captain finished it for her, "They will kill us all."

"How much longer until we reach your friend?"

"We're almost there."

"I hope he's the kind of man we can trust."

"Close enough to one," Seth Cain chuckled as the stars highlighted the red on black tattoos banded across his cheeks and down his squared jawline, "but Bahira is no man. He's a Qabila tribesman. Like the rest of the native species of this planet, they despise humans."

"So do I," Noor grinned, wolfishly.

Cain took a belt from his flask. His breath was spiced with cloves and booze. He wiped his growing beard with the back of his hand and flicked the liquor off his knuckles.

"Did you know this planet wasn't always a desert?" he asked as he offered Noor a belt, but she declined. "A long time ago, Nahl Gul was covered in savannahs, jungles, cataracts, and blue oceans. This world was a garden, but paradises never last long."

"Did we destroy this garden?"

"No. The Malak al-Maut," Cain took another drink, savoring the spice. "When the aliens crashed into the planet, they started a conflict that raged on for over a millennia, turning this world into a barren wasteland." He shook his head, gravely, and gestured at the desert, "We lost this paradise before, Noor; it's our responsibility never to lose it again."

"There is something wrong with this world," Noor snarled.

He spoke the words of the Drus holy book, "All sin stems from man's violence."

"Did the war take your leg, captain?" Noor asked.

He met her gaze. "Enemy steel took it clean off the bone."

"Did you pay the bastards back for it?" She felt a kinship at this talk of enemies.

"That business is done," he kissed his strand of prayer beads, "dead and buried."

"So you understand where I'm coming from?" She sounded desperate for a connection. "You know better than most that nothing matters until we get our revenge."

The captain holstered his shooters, and crossed his arms over his broad chest, "What we want doesn't really matter; the only thing that does is ending this war once and for all."

"I fight for revenge, captain," Noor said. "I don't care who wins at the front."

Cain shook his head. "You have to pick a side. There are no bystanders in war."

"You're right about that, captain. We all get dirty. We all have crimes to pay."

"So you know the truth?" his voice lowered. "We are the monster we seek."

Noor didn't say it; she didn't have to. Everything was clear between them. They saw each other for who they really were. Killers. Noor knew she was a bad woman, but one willing to pay for everything she owed, as long as her enemies gave her the same courtesy.

CHAPTER TWELVE

VALLEY OF THE DEATH ANGELS

Noor powered her night vision scope and zoomed in on the bone-white monoliths, pylons, and ossuaries rising across an open valley. The crumbling structures sunk into the sand dunes, walls torn apart and burned, beams exposed like ribcages. From afar, the Valley of the Death Angels spread out in the shape of a waning moon. The architecture of the necropolis itself was a warning sign for wanderers and grave robbers not to venture any further. The valley was no place for the living; only death loomed beyond this point. Here rested the remains of the legendary alien conquerors of Nahl Gul: the Malak al-Maut.

A whirl of sand kicked up as Noor pulled out her saber. Pure fear pumped through her veins, causing her thumb to hover over the striker with an itch to ignite it. The young Beiji took cover and cowered behind her, muttering a prayer under his tagelmust. He mirrored her movements, taking aim with his rifle into the shadows of the structures ahead. To the west, the Black Dawn was setting beyond the remains of the necropolis.

Starlight swept over the desert, illuminating the sand dunes with the silvered gleam of the night sky.

"I've been to this graveyard before," Noor said. "And I'm in no mood to go back."

"We've lost the cover of darkness; we need to seek shelter," said the captain as he bounded off to a great monolith looming over the other mausoleums and marble pylons.

Noor followed close behind. She went inside, reluctantly, sweating cold, overcome with the feeling she was about to spring some fatal trap. Through the darkness, Noor sensed a presence behind her, something big and nasty and cold. She turned on her heel, swung her saber, and struck it against the stone giant behind her. Noor's sight adjusted to the dark and soon realized she was fighting a pair of scarab statues that guarded the monolith's stairwell; the steps spiraled to the top of the monolith going up, and plunged deep underground going down. Noor peered over the stairwell but couldn't see beyond the first spiral. She bit her lips with the thrill of returning to the scene of a crime.

"Put your steel away." The captain gently lowered her blade. "We're going below."

Noor climbed down the stairwell, counted out her paces on the tiles, and found she could remember every turn and bend of the steps from memory, slipping easily into the ruins like she was coming home. Stone-carved friezes banded the walls and disappeared into the bowels of the monolith. A sequence of primitive chariot battles was engraved into the walls, detailed carvings of the Malak al Maut's legions charging into battle. The panels unfolded in a linear fashion: each slab of marble followed the march of a conquering horde invading the native nations of Nahl Gul; their armies burned cities to rubble, toppled the local's idols, and sacrificed war prisoners on altars made out of an architecture of bones.

At the end of the stairwell, the air thickened with smoke. Noor's boot-heels scraped on the bare bedrock floor. The steps had emptied them into a bunker burrowed deep into the ground. Screwed and bolted into the rock, a ring of sarcophaguses enclosed the walls of the chamber. Noor, knowing exactly where she was, wandered under the shadow of the tombs. She wiped the sweat off her brow, waved through the cloud of smoke, and closed in on the cook fire burning on the other side of the chamber. Poised to strike, she peeled her scimitar halfway out of its scabbard and met the bionic eyes of the figure standing behind the pots and pans. The creature had turned to face her; its lenses glowed a hot red. Its powerful body was hunched over and covered in robes that exposed its talons. A gas mask was fused over the creature's snout, echoing its ragged breathing across the bunker.

This was a desert walker, a native of the Qabila tribesmen, the first peoples of this planet and the keepers of the Valley of the Death Angels. The natives were said to be cut-throat hunters, powerful mystics, and the custodians of the forgotten history of the planet of Nahl Gul. For all the times she had seen them, Noor had never seen one unmasked and alive. Qabila tribesmen covered themselves in gas masks when out in public and only showed their faces among their own kind, a habit born of their distrust for outsiders.

The Qabila raised on its haunches and stood almost four feet taller than an average man. Its cook fire lit up the ivory carapace sweeping the creature's skull like a war helm; this carapace was much sought after in its powdered form as an aphrodisiac in the bazaars of the caliphate's core world, though it was by all rational means an ineffectual remedy.

"Go back to where you came from, outlanders," it said, its sharp talons gleaming near the sputtering cook fire. "This is Qabila land. The tribes of men do not belong here!"

Seth Cain took off his helm, "I come bearing coppers, Bahira, old friend."

"Cain?" The Qabila dropped in an elegant bow. "I thought the war had taken you."

"Not yet." He tossed the creature a bag of coins that it snatched from the air with one swoop of its sharp talons. "My friends and I had a rough landing back in the desert and need a place to stay until sunup. I thought you wouldn't mind the company or the coppers."

"You are all welcome," Bahira's aged voice cracked as it came closer into the light, "to share a meal in my humble warren. Except for that bald animal following behind you."

"You got a problem with me, old timer?" Noor asked.

The Qabila's bionic eyes glared at her. "Fedayeen blood reeks off you."

"You're wrong," she said. "I walked away from that path a long time ago."

"Bah!" Bahira scraped its talons on the ground. "It doesn't much matter whether you bind to a live sun or a dead one, all of you star fire binders smell the same to me. Your kind were the greatest plague to befall the first peoples of Nahl Gul. The Fedayeen invaders almost burned my entire tribe to extinction. They enslaved the noble jackals and drove the bug queens underground. Your kind is a terrible plague. Now, you have doomed us all!"

All in all, Noor brooded, silently, not wanting to give Bahira the satisfaction, she knew it was right. "Don't worry," she winked. "I'm in no mood for genocide tonight."

The Qabila turned back to the fire and raised the lid on the pot. A brew of insect shells, scorpions, blood sausages, and tubers bubbled to the surface of the greasy gumbo. Noor's mouth watered, but not without shame. The scorpion legs looked fresh and tender. She could nearly taste the salt and sizzling fat dripping off the spicy goat-blood sausages. Hunger won over her suspicions. She followed the others and scrubbed her hands with the grated sand on a traditional Qabila ablution bowl before beginning their supper. Noor slurped at her bowl and wolfed down the gumbo. The captain cracked open a scorpion leg and sucked out the meat. Kamal didn't touch the food; his bowl went cold as he huddled in the back of the bunker, his eyes fixed on the creature behind the cook fire. The desert walker chuckled at the kid with a wheezing cough and spooked him back against the wall.

"What are you so scared of, boy?" Bahira asked.

"These friends of yours?" he asked, pointing to the tombs looming over him.

"Your Fedayeen were not the first invaders to covet this planet," the Qabila said. "A millennia before the crusaders came, the Malak al Maut almost brought down the heavens. The conquerors' great horde warred over control of Nal Ghul in an endless conflict that almost destroyed this planet and every living creature on it. But my ancestors defeated the aliens and built these monoliths to entomb their spirits inside before they could kill us all."

"Who did you bury here?"

"She has many names," Bahira said. "One for every world she devoured. The Night Mother and her children conquered every nation under our red sun to cast this world into darkness. The Malak al-Maut are sun eaters who travelled across the galaxy draining power from the stars, preaching an end of day's cult and offering fanatics a paradise of the night."

Without warning, the Qabila tribesman dislodged the sarcophagus from the bunker's walls and brought it thundering to the ground. Bahira then pried open the lid with its sharp talons, and revealed the empty tomb hidden underneath the heavy, stone slab.

"The alien's been set loose," Bahira pointed at Noor, "by the hands of that woman!" The creature jumped on her, closed its sharp talon around her neck, and squeezed tight. "Desert justice demands that you be scourged and crucified for what you have done."

Seth Cain tried to step between them but got tossed backwards by the Qabila.

"She's a monster," Noor croaked, struggling against his grip, "but irresistible."

"And you fell for her game hook and sinker."

"I tried to put her down," she said. "But I failed. I won't make that mistake again."

Bahira let her go, dropping her on the ground. "You're not the hero of this story."

"No." She spat out wad of blood. "Not even close."

"What have you done?" the captain asked Noor from across the bunker.

Bahira answered for her. "She released the devil from its cage."

"My unit was sent here on a mission." Her words poured out like a confession. "The mullahs wanted the monoliths of the Malak al Maut razed and the alien's tombs set alight. I led my unit into the Valley of the Death Angels and started burning everything in sight, but when I set foot into this crypt, a strange voice called out to me from inside that coffin. It was something like magnetism, an unstoppable attraction. I had no choice but to open it...

"Inside, I found something strange, a cloud of black smoke moving as if alive. It spoke to me and offered to reveal the great revelation of the galaxy. A paradise of the night. I can't say I wasn't curious. Who doesn't want to uncover the mysteries of our time? Surprising myself, I gave in to caution and first refused her, but the phantom wasn't taking no for an answer. The black smoke lunged straight for me, but my beloved Khadija stepped in its path. The phantom burrowed into her eyes, nostrils, and screaming mouth. Khadija was no longer herself after that moment. Whatever she had become, it wasn't human.

"This creature offered us power, enlightenment, and freedom from the mullahs. It was a tempting offer for any slave soldier. Every single one of the warriors in my unit took it. She led us to the capitol that same night to start a war and burn down the Star Fire Temple. I killed more than my own share of Fedayeen that night. My hands are bloodier than most. By the time she cast a spell to devour the sun it was too late for me to stop her."

"Why did you follow her?" Bahira asked.

"Because I loved her, even if she was a monster." Her voice hardened. "I failed my duty the last time, but nothing will stop me now. The Night Mother will burn by my hand."

The Qabila stepped back to the cook fire, tossing his spotted mutts the scraps and leavings from the pot; the dogs fought for every piece of gristle, goat-sausage, and bone.

Bahira went quiet for a long while before he spoke. "How did you do it?"

"Did what?"

"How did you try to kill her?"

"I stabbed her in the back," Noor smiled like a wolf, reliving the memory.

"Dark fire made the Night Mother and only it can burn her phantom back to the other side." The desert walker got up on its haunches and went off into an unlit passage of the monolith's bunker. "But be careful killing monsters lest you become one yourself...

"You will all die, but not here, not now – I want you out before the Black Dawn."

* * *

The Qabila stood at the gates of the monolith, decked in a white, flowing robe that snaked in folds on the sand, its red, bionic eyes gleamed with the fading starlight. Noor had shrouded her bald head and blacked out her face, turning anonymous under her burnouse. She raised her night scope and tracked the lens across the horizon of the sprawling valley.

"What is it that you think you'll find out there?" Bahira asked her.

"Nothing but death."

"I hope you find it," the creature said.

The Qabila shut the rusted gate with a thud and bolted the locks.

Noor turned her back on the monolith and wandered across the ruins of the necropolis. The crumbling tombs spread out around her with no end in sight. As she dug her boots into the sand, a strange sense of foreboding swept over her and turned her breath cold. She started to mutter something like a prayer, but quickly managed to stop herself.

Kamal walked up to her, rifle slung over his shoulder. "What now?"

"We run," Noor said, gunning it across the ruins.

CHAPTER THIRTEEN

THE BURNING WOMAN

Dawn. The dark sun rose from the east, feeding off starlight, a black scarab devouring the horizon. Darkness bled over the sand dunes, covering the Night Mother's trail as she rode across the desert. She pulled the reins of her pale mare and brought it to a stop less than half a klick from a caravan traveling on the old highway. Drus tribes pulled overloaded carts with pack reptiles, following a column of hundreds of refugees. The elders and merchants rode on caparison-draped horses, kicking up sand on the vanguard. Every woman and girl straggled at the back with the cattle. A trail of the sick and dying were left behind to fend on their own. These refugees were on a rootless migration around the world, scavenging the desert for hot springs to share in the residual heat of the planetary core.

The Mother removed her veil and let her curls wave with the wind. Her milky eyes fixed on a young woman left behind by the caravan, drifting into the outback on her own. She was a tribeswoman from the clans of the cataracts by the color of her blue robes and the tattoos covering her face and every inch of her body. The tribeswoman was skinny and barefoot. A hive-spotted toddler squealed in her arms, barely old enough to waddle on its own two legs. She carried her daughter across a field strewn with carcasses of crawler tanks and downed aircraft, reached the edge of a tar pit, and dropped on her knees to pray.

A scree of sand and debris rose as the Night Mother spurred her mare and galloped to the steaming pit, close enough to feel heat on her skin. She nodded to the tribeswoman.

"What do you pray for?" She dismounted and knelt by her side.

"Please..." The tribeswoman begged, tears streaming the arabesque tattoos inked around her eyes. "Help us. My little girl's sick. We got nowhere to go in the darkness."

The Night Mother cooed at the toddler, "She won't make it past nightfall."

"I don't believe you!" The tribeswoman blessed herself, pulling her daughter away.

"There's only one way that you can give her peace, but it is a hard path."

The tribeswoman covered her mouth as if she was about to wretch, realizing what the strange rider was asking her. "I didn't carry her in belly to bury her body in the sand."

"There are worse things you can do to your own than violence. You can't see it now, but this is what a mother's mercy looks like."

"I could never survive without her. She's a part of me. If she dies, I go with her."

"If you can't live without her, then you must follow after her to the other side."

"What do you know about the other side?" the tribeswoman snapped.

"Do you think I don't know grief?" The Night Mother unholstered her plated guns. "I've spawned thousands of warriors, handsome sons, and terrible monsters only to watch them die, rotting in a tomb. My own

hands have shut their eyes closed to spare them pain. But soon, when that dying star finally goes black forever, my dear sons will return to me."

"I want to believe," the tribeswoman muttered.

"Then renounce your false religion, let go of the material world, and set yourselves free. All you have to do is die. A paradise of the night will await you on the other side."

"Will I see her again," the tribeswoman asked, cautiously, "in paradise?"

"No," the Night Mother said, coldly.

The tribeswoman bent over her daughter, cleaning her hive-spotted skin with the traditional sand ablutions customary to her clan until the girl was clean of sweat and bile. She binded her little body with rags, tying her arms and legs together, and kissed her forehead. Obsidian stones covered the girl's eyes when she dipped her into the pool of tar until she stopped breathing. The tribeswoman pulled the still bundle out of the pit, dripping hot gobs of tar. She held her daughter close to her, a skeleton face nuzzled at her breast.

She took two steps into the pit, and turned back to the rider, swallowing a scream, "I don't see anything." Her voice was cracked, beginning to fill with panic and self-doubt.

"Oh, but you will," The Night Mother raised her pistols and scorched out the tribeswoman's eyes—the bullets ignited a wave of crackling flames that swept her over. The blaze surged as if their twisted bodies were dancing on the shores of the tar pit.

"Now," she said to her mare, mounting back on the saddle, "she can finally see."

A growing bonfire swept up into the sky as the Night Mother looked back on the tar pit and spurred her mare into a full gallop, speeding away on the main road to the capitol.

CHAPTER FOURTEEN

LAST STOP TO THE END OF THE WORLD

The desert crossing split into a fork in the road. Four broken obelisks marked the planet's cardinal points and the dividing line of the equator. Noor sat on top of one of the broken pillars, the captain and the Beiji were taking a breather below her swinging boots. In the distance, a hulking transport barreled through the desert, kicking up a cloud of sand and dust, picking up speed as it careened on the road. The ground shook under the rig's tracks as it came to a stop in front of the crossings. Its exhausts belched and rained down soot all over Noor. The cargo doors lurched open to an outdated service droid bowing behind the wheel. A holographic skin warped over its blank head, toggling between hundreds of faces until it settled on that of a sunken-eyed, cackling crone, "Last stop to the end of the world."

Noor jumped from her place on the broken pillar and followed the captain and the Beiji up the rig's creaking ramp, paying for their passage. The droid toggled its face to that of a handsome soldier and winked at Noor as if they knew each other intimately. She boarded the cargo hold and pushed her way through the passengers. Hundreds of refugees huddled together with their different tribes in the belly of the rig. Dealers sold dime-bags of blue poppy in one corner. Beiji dancers stripped for coins in the back. A pack of jackals mauled each other for the entertainment of gamblers hooting for more action and blood.

Noor left Cain and Kamal by the fights and went off to roam the rig on her own, her body working on fumes, blinking in and out of awareness. She needed a drink, badly.

A second service droid was making the rounds in the cargo hold pushing a rolling cart, selling dates, bug carapaces, and shots of starshine. Noor stuck her fingers in her mouth and whistled to get the scrap metal rescue's attention. It powered up its headlights, and headed straight for her. When it got to her, she tossed the droid a handful of coppers, and it poured her a shot of smoking starshine. She knocked back the hooch in a single glug, and tapped her coin on the barkeep for another. Nahl Gul starshine was high-grade and only had a whiff of the stink of ethyl. In her opinion and that of anyone else with taste, it was of a finer quality than any of the swill imported from the Celestial Caliphate's core world.

But one drink never did it for her. Noor was no stranger to over-indulgence. She gave the droid half of her purse and snatched an uncorked bottle from the cart. It was worth every damned coin. Noor grinned, flicked the droid off, and walked on into the crowd.

The crowd thinned out near the toilets. Noor popped the cork from the bottle and drank, greedily, downing it in six champion glugs. She pushed her head out the window and breathed in the night air, gazing out into the sandstone ruins and high-rises of an abandoned Drus city that disappeared from the line of the horizon. Noor narrowed her eyes on the crumbling structures in the distance and watched them slowly fade away and vanish.

Weaving, she stumbled around drunk with a burned-out match hanging from her lips, eyeballing the hundreds of refugees packed in the cargo hold, flapping open her burnouse to show off the steel she had packing to anyone that looked at her too long. She knew that her nerves were frayed as buckets of sweat slid down her head. The ghosts of her enemies were hunting after her, even in every dark corner of this rig – this she knew for sure. A cold sense of foreboding made her shudder. The danger seemed imminent. Something was out there and it was hunting her. Suddenly, Noor felt alone and exposed.

Feeling exhausted, she tried to stay awake, but her heavy drinking knocked her out cold. Her head hit the floor with a thud as she succumbed to the pull of an ethyl blackout.

*   *   *

Noor woke up in a daze. Her head was pounding, her tongue fat and bone-dry. Paranoia took her over as she felt the heat of a stranger closing in. Instinctively, she gripped the neck of the bottle and swung, breaking it against the captain's helmet. Seth Cain cried out and pushed her back against the wall, elbow pressed firmly against her gulping throat.

"What in Hell is wrong with you, woman?" Cain asked.

Noor wiped the drunken sweat off her head and shrugged. She'd always had a sharp tongue, a short fuse, and a talent for stumbling into a brawl. Violence came too easy for her.

"Sorry, captain, bad dreams."

"We're here," Seth Cain said. "The capitol is only a few kilometers south."

The loudspeakers scratched across the cargo hold as the rig sped up on the road. "Last stop to our final destination. Samarak. The city of one thousand silver minarets."

Noor's eyes dilated with fear. "We're not going to make it. Something is out there."

"You're drunk."

"Maybe," she said. "But that doesn't mean I'm wrong."

"Trust me." Cain blessed himself. "Star fire will protect us."

"You don't really believe in that old religion, do you?"

Seth Cain turned his icy eyes on Noor and placed his hand over her shoulder, gently, "Only star fire makes the galaxy go round. Its plasma binds us all together. Every lifeform is born from a spark of solar fusion and burns back to it in the end. Even you."

She cackled out loud. There was no sense in arguing with a fanatic about his religion. Noor was on a low down killing spree and she had no more time for bullshit.

Noor lit up a smoke and pulled Cain close, faces inches apart, his breathe hot on her skin. "I want to know everything. It's been a long time since I've been to the front."

Seth Cain plucked the cigarillo hanging from her lips and collected the ash in his meaty palms. He dabbed his fingers in the ashes and drew a crude map on the floors of the cargo hold. A long, winding line of soot separated the sketch into two opposing camps.

"The mullahs and their armies are in control of the west bank," he said. "The Night Mother's forces are holed up behind the great Kasbah and control everything to the east."

"It's a stalemate," she muttered.

"The alien and the Fallen are the few," Cain said, "but the mullah's armies are the many. Trust in the star's fire. It has been foreseen. All of the faith's enemies will burn."

"And we'll roast with them!" Noor cackled, pointing out the windows.

Overhead, a roaring gunship sped across the sky, its rotary canons aimed on the rig.

Sadira Rah's gunship opened fire, striking the belly of the transport. An explosion tore through the engines. The blast tossed the hulking rig off the ground, flipped it over on its back, and crashed the bow into the sand dunes. Smoke columned from the wreckage.

CHAPTER FIFTEEN

WELCOME HOME

Fall-out rained down on Noor as she broke through the remains of the cargo doors. The survivors trickled out of the rig, carrying the dead and wounded outside. Most refugees in the back of the transport made it out alive, but those packed in the front weren't so lucky.

Back on the ground, Noor scanned the desert for signs of the gunship, but Sadira Rah had disappeared into the outback. She dusted herself off. That was a close call. She got herself back on the road and blended in with the rest of the refugees travelling on foot, approaching Samarak's city limits. A smile creased her cheeks. She was coming home.

On the queue to the main gates, she spotted the Beiji's mop of brown curls. Kamal and Cain looked scraped but well enough. Both were buying sugared dates from a vendor.

Kamal elbowed the captain. "She's back from the dead."

"Welcome back." Cain nibbled on a date. "Luck's on your side."

"We'll see about that," she said. "Let's get the action started."

Noor waited for the captain to finish his dates and then followed him into the city. Artillery fire lit up the streets of the capitol—bombed out high-rises, a thousand broken minarets, and the walls of the great Kasbah of Samarak stretched out across the skyline. Noor trained her eyes on a temple perched above the surrounding volcanic range. She shook her head. This was not the home she remembered. There was nothing left but bones.

A muezzin's call to prayer echoed through the streets and called out to Noor with something like seduction. She followed a crowd of the faithful to the front of a temple on the corner of Dei Boulevard. Noor waded through the crowd. Smoke spilled out onto the street from the ceremonial pyre burning inside. Cannon guns loomed atop the minarets. The prayers to the stars echoed out over the loudspeakers. Noor couldn't stop herself from mouthing the words, bowing, and turning east to meet the rise of the Black Dawn. The rituals came back like instinct, but they no longer worked for her. The heat, her old connection to the star's fire was gone. She'd lost that spark long before the sun went out.

To the faithful, Noor was an unbeliever – a *kafir* – a wanderer from the faith. She had fallen from grace and turned her back on her own religion. There was no going back.

The captain slipped through the crowd, gripped the nook of her arm, and cocked his helm towards the shelled buildings lining the flophouse district. "It's time," he said. Noor turned her back on the temple and her old religion once again. She followed the captain through the busy street to the courtyard of a dusty caravanserai packed with a string of eateries, teahouses, dancing joints, and cut throat cantinas on the ground floor.

Noor eyed the street rats hanging about the corner, and peeled out a few inches of her scimitar to warn off the pocket thieves; they got the message and melted into the crowd.

"It's almost over; wait for me in the tea-house," the captain said.

Noor rolled her eyes. "I'm tired of waiting."

"Trust me," he said, hiding his face under his helm and walking out into the street.

Noor wandered around the courtyard of the caravanserai. She spotted a rabble of soldiers hooting and tossing coins at a dancer stripping on the sidewalk. The sun-starved boy moved his hips in slow, teasing gyrations, slinking off his colored veils, and playing scarab-bone castanets, his oiled body glistening with the lights of explosions blossoming in the sky. Kamal fought to get in front of the rest of the crowd and take a front row seat for the show. He stared at the other boy with lusty eyes, his mouth dropped wide open.

"He's too rich for your blood, kid," Noor heckled from the back of the crowd.

"We'll see about that!" The Beiji threw the dancer a handful of coppers. The stripper shed a single, sequined veil, and winked back at him. Kamal was on the hook.

Noor grinned, left the kid to try his luck with the dancer, and pushed through the beaded curtains of the teahouse, a shady watering hole on the back-end of the ground floor. She walked into the parlor just as another explosion rocked the city; the gas chandeliers and knee-high tables shook, but none of the patrons blinked at the low impact blast. The smell of coriander, molasses, and spice transported her far from the hellhole outside. Her eyes swept through the space from left and then to the right. A group of veterans were huddled by the bar, playing a game of dice. Fat boys with rich daddies feasted on a roasted beetle carapace. Bearded men swaddled in furs drank smoke from the tentacles of a large, smoldering narguile. The women and girls were separated behind a honeycombed partition in the back, to rest, and pray, and keep among their own, just as the Drus religion required.

A couple of soldiers whistled and catcalled at Noor from across the parlor; but they went dead quiet when her black-veined, skeletal face came into the light. Then the men averted their gaze in shame and revulsion. Nothing new to Noor; she cowled herself, and slipped into a private room in the back of the teahouse. Inside, she nestled into a pile of plush pillows and spotted animal hides, and finally, for the first time in days, relaxed.

The curtains to the room swept open and a waitress bowed into the room; she approached a knee-high table and poured hot water into a porcelain bowl, preparing lotus flower tea. Noor slurped the crimson brew, chewed on the lotus flower and swallowed it.

"Not bad..." she smacked her lips

The waitress bowed, meek, playing at obeisance, retreating slowly from the room. She was giggling, covering a grin that was all gums and no teeth with the back of her hand.

Noor sat back on the cushions and propped her feet on the table, knocking over the porcelain bowl. She felt tired. Sleep was shutting her eyes. Suddenly, the room started spinning like she'd overdosed on poppy again, even though she hadn't smoked for hours. Panic hit. Noor quickly realized she wasn't alone. In fact, she was completely surrounded.

A pack of armed men stormed into the room. The captain and a ring of soldiers armed with assault rifles surrounded her, aiming for kill-shots. A trap closed around her.

"Welcome home." Cain drew a scimitar and ignited it in red-hot flames.

CHAPTER SIXTEEN

THE FEDAYEEN ORDER

Noor woke up with a boot to the face. Her eyes opened to a Drus temple. Seth Cain sent her body rolling to the foot of a mob of monks, soldiers, and Fedayeen warriors gathered in front a ceremonial pyre. She spat out blood and tried to push herself up, but the mob around her took turns kicking her back to the floor. Helpless, all Noor could do was flick off the snickering men looming over her. She hadn't seen this many warriors of the order since that first massacre at the Star Fire Temple and the start of the Black Dawn.

Three fat, old clerics watched her bleed from behind the pyre. The great mullahs of the colony of Nahl Gul sat on their plush thrones, tended by a cadre of gelded slaves and dervishes. The holy men were covered in gold-trimmed, flowing kaftans, their faces hidden behind porcelain masks. Their bodies were known to be covered in scabs, boils, and radiation burns, the mark of the natives from the Drus core world's shattered atmosphere.

Seth Cain took off his helmet and bowed before the three mullahs, "Your divine graces, this woman is my gift for you; the second most wanted of the Fallen Fedayeen."

"Second most wanted," Noor scoffed. "Who beat me to the top spot?"

"Only the devil herself." Cain decked her to shut her up.

Seth Cain nicked Noor's own scimitar under her chin, forced her to her knees, and paraded her in front of the mullahs' thrones. The crowd hooted and went wild as she shook her shackles, bared her teeth, and snarled. She would play along with Cain's little show. For now. The prayer hall went quiet as a lone figure cloaked in a crimson robe walked across the temple with the aid of a probing, bamboo cane. Soldiers stood to attention as he walked past them. The Fedayeen fell to their knees. Every gawker in his path gained way.

Maalik Raj, grand master of the Fedayeen Order, bowed at Noor. His blind eyes were banded in red and ivory silk that gave the effect of a bleeding wound. Raj had trained Noor as a star fire binder and a crusader of the faith, turning her into a weapon for the caliphate, a slave soldier with a fire sword. But Noor had never been a good slave to religion. Chained animals always snap, break their leash, and bite the hand that feeds them.

"You have returned to us, my long, lost child." Maalik Raj blessed himself.

Noor couldn't meet the old man's blind gaze. "Hello, master," she muttered.

"You're on the wrong side of the Kasbah." His fingers traced the veins on her head. "The rest of the Fallen Fedayeen stand with the alien squatting in our Star Fire Temple."

Noor bucked against her scimitar. The edge nicked her throat and dripped a trickle of blood down her cleavage. "You got it all wrong. I don't fight for any side but my own!"

"Why would I trust a woman that compacted with the devil?" Maalik Raj asked.

"My eyes didn't see a devil," Noor admitted. "To me, she was the woman I loved. But I was wrong. I saw what I wanted to see. Khadija was gone. Only a monster remained."

"My poor, lost child, you want forgiveness, but you won't get it." His voice boomed across the temple. "You have binded to a dead star, turned your back on your religion, attacked its holy sites, and killed scores of your own kind. It is too late. The die is cast."

Seth Cain raised the saber over her head. "On your command, master," he said.

"Do it!" Noor screamed.

"Stay your hand," Maalik Raj ordered. "Their divine graces will decide her fate."

Cain hedged but followed orders, dropping Noor back on her knees. He nuzzled his lips into her ear, and whispered, "Careful losing that pretty bald head."

Maalik Raj approached the old men sitting on their thrones as they consulted the augurs of the flames burning atop their scepters. The mullahs conferred amongst themselves and shared what they saw in the fire to Raj alone. The grand master bowed to the mullahs and turned to Noor. He slammed his cane on the ground to silence the temple.

"Their divine graces are in the mood for mercy, but they want something in return."

"The end of the world brings out the worst in us." Noor winked at Seth Cain.

"The battle for the capital is stalemated," Maalik Raj leaned on his cane "No side has had a breakthrough for months. But that may all change by the next planetary rotation. The army of the faithful are preparing an assault to overwhelm the defenders of the Kasbah. The chaos will make it possible for a skilled warrior like you to slip through the battle unnoticed, make your way to the Star Fire Temple, find the Night Mother, and kill her."

Noor grinned, "So, the mullahs want their rogue weapon back in their arsenal?"

"Do you accept their divine graces generous offer?" Maalik Raj asked.

"Sure," she croaked. "You need a devil on your side if you want to win this war."

"Master," Cain interrupted, "this woman's a criminal. Remember, she helped burn down the Star Fire Temple and hunted after our brothers and sisters. We can't trust her."

"Don't get between me and killing," Noor snarled. "I've nothing to lose!"

Maalik Raj drew a hidden blade from his cane. Red flames skipped on the steel as he aimed the fiery edge on Noor. "There's no trusting a kaffir; that's why Cain's going with you. Thank their divine graces, my poor, lost child. You're very lucky to be alive."

Noor gripped the edge of her scimitar, bled on the steel, and tore it away from Seth Cain. She licked at the red gash in her palm, "Funny...I don't feel lucky."

CHAPTER SEVENTEEN

LET'S GO TO WAR

The cannon atop the minaret spun around with a scatter of sparks. Noor lounged on the gunner's seat, boots propped on the shields, grinding gears and speeding the artillery piece's rotations. She cackled, guzzling a bottle of spiced starshine. With a sudden jerk, she pulled a lever, and grinded the cannon to a screeching halt. Her eyes zeroed in on the sprawling Kasbah caught dead in her sights. The Kasbah stretched out across the city and sealed off the eastern districts of the capitol; its scorched walls and gunner turrets looked impenetrable. Noor lit up a smoke. She worked the gun's levers, aimed the high-caliber barrel, and mock fired a salvo at the citadel. Her dark lips mouthed the phantom boom.

She switched her sights on to night vision. In the Kasbah, thousands of soldiers packed the battlements. Seeing those numbers, cold fear hit her hard as it all started to become real. She took a belt for courage and burned her cigarillo to a smoldering nub.

Across the sky, ships and cruisers took off and glided into the planet's lower orbit. Noor had always wanted to rocket out of this rock, sail through space, and lose herself deep in the galaxy. But even as a child she never thought it would really happen. All her dreams still seemed remote and their final destination completely out of her reach. Behind her, footsteps echoed from the minaret's ladder. Noor turned back from the gun and drew her saber out, hovering the steel over the young Beiji's head. The kid backed up to the rails.

"Never sneak up on a woman with a gun between her legs." Noor puffed out a cloud of smoke straight into Kamal's face. "That's just asking for a world of trouble, kid."

He looked ashen and grim. "Is it true? Are we going to war?"

"That's right." She nodded her bald head and pulled on the bottle.

"You're finally going to get your revenge."

"Maybe..." she muttered, afraid of wanting something, and then finally getting it.

"What about my vengeance?" Kamal asked. "You still owe me my brother's life."

Noor nodded, quietly. The Beiji was right, but she couldn't say the words out loud.

"You can't survive the end of days, but you can leave behind your mark." She turned to the cannon. "Believe me, I'll pay back everything I owe when the war's over."

"And I will be there by your side." Kamal gripped his rifle.

"Skip out of town, kid. You're too young to die in this war. Wait for the next one."

"You don't understand," he said. "I'm going to war with you so you don't come back alive. You are my kill, Noor. Mine! Only death pays for justice in this tomb world."

The Beiji's knuckles went white on his rifle's forestock. Kamal looked sick with rage and bloodlust. He was turning into a killer, slow but sure. Noor met his eyes and saw them mirror back her own. No doubt about it; they were both doomed. She tried to caress the kid's face, but he pulled away. The rejection stung her deeper than she thought it would.

"Don't let obsession consume you like it did me. It'll only take you to a bad place."

"This nightmare." Tears streaked down Kamal's cheeks. "How long does it last?"

"Until all your enemies are dead," she said, simply.

"Do you really believe that?"

Noor aimed the cannon's sights on the turrets of the Kasbah. She knew the answer that Kamal needed, the lie that would protect him, but she told him the hard truth, instead.

"Revenge will be yours, if you have the patience for it," she sighed. "I promised you my life in exchange for the one I took from you, and it's yours after the war is over; but when you take it from me, don't expect my death to bring you peace. Nothing ever will."

"We'll see," Kamal slung his rifle on his shoulder and took off down the ladder.

Noor sighed. Her long journey was close to the end. Khadija was near. She could feel it. This, finally, was their moment. It was now or never. For years now, she had dreamed of meeting her beloved and roasting her to ash. Noor wasn't the hero Khadija needed. No one was coming to save her. All Noor knew how to do was slash and burn.

She dismounted the cannon just as Seth Cain climbed up the minaret's ladder to meet her. Cain packed his shooters in one, quick cross-wise move. The Fedayeen removed his helmet; the jet on crimson bars tattooed on his face were hidden by a wild, black beard.

He turned to the east and the rising darkness. "It's almost time," he said.

"You got gall to face me armed and drunk, 'captain'. You owe me a sucker punch."

"Do your worst," Cain smiled. "But of all people, you can't fault me for betrayal."

"Let's get this over with." She traced the bullet scars under her clothes. "I'm ready."

"I've just received a report that might be of interest," Cain said. "The Fallen Fedayeen you're looking for, Sistani Amin, commands the armies defending the Kasbah."

Noor threw her head back and cackled, "Oh, I've been looking forward to this."

She joined Cain at the minaret's steps. A crooked grin crawled up her face as she head butted the Fedayeen and dropped him like a stone down to the street below. Cain rolled around on the concrete, holding his nose together, and spitting out gobs of blood.

Noor's bald head dripped, slick and red, "Let's go to war."

CHAPTER EIGHTEEN

KILLING FIELD

Noor waited on the lip of the mud-caked trenches and trained her carbine's crosshairs on the dying star rising over the walls of Samarak's great Kasbah. Black veins tiger-striped across her skin as she primed herself for a fight in the darkness. The rags of her robes shrouded over her gear, the gun, scimitar, a breastplate, and two bandoliers that crossed over her cleavage with blinking frag grenades. The mullahs' soldiers, packed into the grid of underground trenches, went quiet. Silence stretched out, time slowed, almost stopped, letting the tension build. Breathing heavy, they gripped their guns and prayer beads, and shuffled through the tunnel system to take their attack positions. From a distance, the muezzin's first call to prayer echoed across the city. That was the signal.

Noor levelled the carbine in front of her eyes, shot a live round into the air as a war cry, and charged out of the trenches with the first wave of soldiers. A maelstrom of shrapnel, fallout, and ash whirled across the smoke-filled battle ground. Artillery fire strafed down from the Kasbah and boomed all around her.

She pushed through the cloud of debris and hurled herself into the path of the enemy. Noor aimed dead ahead—mowing down a squadron of incoming suicide-fighters; the men's corpses carbonized to the bone inside their fire-bomb armors. She moved through the rising smoke sweeping her carbine's barrel, enemy soldiers materializing across her line of sight, caught in the crosshairs. She gnashed her teeth, squeezed the trigger and plugged the frontline units into the ground.

War ululations echoed all around her. Noor's boots dug into the broken concrete as gunners surrounded her in a half-circle—execution style. She grinned at them as they opened fire. Noor vaulted into the air, ignited her scimitar, and landed behind the gunners; she swung her steel, and lopped off every one of their heads in a single swipe as she ran around their backs, faster than they could turn around and find out what was happening to them. As the men fell, like marionettes whose strings were cut, a grin crawled up Noor's blood-splattered face. The explosions of war rose up behind her. All across the Kasbah, the mullah's armies were on the move as they stormed against the fighters defending the wall. Counter-fire intensified and bodies piled up, the killing field only growing by the minute.

A barrage of rockets detonated and shook the ground beneath her. Noor's heart skipped a beat as she spotted the crawler tanks lumbering out from behind the city walls on their mechanical legs, shooting a salvo of mortars from their turrets. Noor pumped lead into one of the crawlers until her carbine burned hot, locked, and cashed out. It did nothing. The carbine was no match against the tank's armor. She tossed the gun over her shoulder and sized up the crawlers. If Noor couldn't destroy them she would use them to her advantage.

Running towards it, the crawler turned on her and lobbed a round of rockets her way. She ducked in a snap and scudded low to the ground just as the mortars peeled off and exploded behind her. When she got to the tank's base, she climbed up its legs and carapace, ran across the length of its spine, and jumped high into the air, swooping over the Kasbah walls. She landed on the muzzle of an artillery cannon, slid down the length of its barrel, and sprung over the battlements. Noor braced herself with her blade lit up in dark flames.

Enemy soldiers circled around her, aiming their rifles at Noor's head. She slowly backtracked to the battlements and looked down on the long drop from the Kasbah. Noor swallowed hard when she heard the sound of heavy boots and a booming laughter. Sistani Amin pushed through the soldiers like a charging wildebeest of the hamada, flinging his own men who stood in his way over the walls. The corpulent warrior bowed, mockingly, at Noor; a pair of scimitars, a collection of daggers, shanks, automatics, and nickel-plated pistols were holstered on the belt of horrors holding in his belly. Staring down at her, Sistani Amin took off his turbaned helmet and smiled. The ugly corkscrew scar Noor had given him the last time they'd fought ran deep from his forehead to his chin. Oily veins sprawled over his black skin and circled around the one good eye her scimitar had left him.

"Stand down!" Amin barked at his soldiers. "This one is all mine."

"I want you too, big guy." Noor winked at him. "And I want you bad."

"Surrender, unbeliever, or there will be more violence."

"Joke's on you," she said. "Violence is the only pleasure left in a dying world."

Sistani Amin unsheathed his double-bladed scimitars and ignited them. He slashed the blades, trailed by sweeps of dark fire, charging straight at her. The scimitars singed across her bald head as she dodged and weaved away from the weapons. Noor leapt back onto the battlements, met Amin's one eye, and swung for his head, but the Fallen Fedayeen moved quicker than she remembered, juiced up on the dead star's energy. He parried the blow with one saber and decked her across the mouth with the hilt of the other, downing her body to the ground. Noor struggled on all fours and gnashed broken teeth at the Fallen.

Amin put out his scimitars and sheathed them. His belly jiggled as he laughed, making the guns and blades on his belt clank and jangle. He offered her a doughy hand.

"Beg for the Night Mother's mercy," he said, "and she will grant it."

"I know what her mercy looks like," Noor croaked.

"Death is the only way to see paradise." Sistani Amin wrapped his gauntlets around Noor's neck and squeezed her windpipe closed, building up a painful pressure in her skull. "Do you see it yet?" The Fallen Fedayeen asked, digging his thumbs under her jawbone.

"No," she said, driving her saber into his boots, "but you're about to."

Sistani Amin let go of her neck and staggered backwards, bringing down several of his soldiers. Noor shot her blade like a boomerang, slicing through the air in quick, sudden reels. The steel broke through Amin's armor under his arm and drove deep into his ribs. He dropped to his knees, clutched the scimitar running through him, and pulled the length out.

The big guy tossed Noor's weapon back at her and spat out a spray of blood.

"Just a scratch!" the Fallen roared. "You are unworthy of Night Mother's love."

"No doubt," she snickered, "but I've picked up one of her tricks."

Noor dropped on her shoulder and rolled to Sistani Amin's side; she swiped a nickel-plated pistol from his belt of horrors and shot a slug into his one good eye—tunneling a hole through his skull that let through the light from the artillery fire overhead.

Sistani Amin's soldiers backed away from her as their general fell. Noor waved at them and tossed a couple of blinking grenades at their feet; the explosions were blinding and ripped through the Kasbah battlements, blowing the ring of enemy fighters to pieces.

Noor hurled backwards with the impact. Flames burned holes through her burnouse and kameez. Shrapnel skidded across the ground and dug deep into the meat of her calf.

She limped back on her feet, wading through the smoke and debris, moving in slow motion, her vision distorted, ears ringing, legs shaking from the shrapnel. She avoided walking over the skeleton pieces of the soldiers and peered down over the crumbling walls. Artillery and rocket fire shook the great Kasbah. Siege towers crashed against the battlements. A detonation breached the gates and brought down the citadel's main defenses. The walls came down in waves, the enemy soldiers scattered, and chaos spread everywhere. The mullah's armies broke through the walls and spilled into the citadel. A squadron of janissary troopers moved in formation, shields interlocked into an impenetrable square. Seth Cain and the Beiji emerged from the huddle of soldiers. The kid blessed himself as he took in the horrifying number of corpses and kept his rifle aimed at anything that moved.

"Look at this place." The kid turned white as a ghost.

Cain, hearing this, wandered the battlements with a smile. "Yes, this is what victory looks like, kid," he said. "The Kasbah has fallen just like their divine graces had foreseen."

Noor picked up her scimitar and blew out the fire snaking over the steel.

"The Black Dawn's not over yet," she warned.

CHAPTER NINETEEN

ONLY TERROR WILL KEEP YOU ALIVE

"It's almost over," Noor muttered, her words silenced by the roar of another blast – a series of explosions reverbed outside the Kasbah, shaking the great citadel's foundations. She left the medic's station behind after the surgeons removed the shrapnel from her leg, warning her about a massive infection and internal bleeding, but she shrugged them off. All she needed was drugs for the pain, once the opiates faded she'd welcome coming undone. Around her, soldiers filled the hallways. Bleeding, limbless men were carried away in gurneys. Prisoners were hastily executed on their knees. Body thieves stole away the corpses of the dead. The stench of burning flesh filled the air as Noor shuffled away from the pandemonium and receded into an abandoned prayer hall at the end of the corridor.

The hall was dim, muggy, and stank of decay. Spider webs, grime, and thick coats of dust covered the pews, altar, and the honeycombed partition that separated the sexes. This place hadn't seen worship for many years, another ruin of the old world. Across the room, she spotted a lone, unlit oil lamp swinging from the ceiling to the beat of the wind currents. She approached it, where beyond it everything was swallowed by the darkness of the room. Noor lit the wick with the strike of a match. She grinned as it sparked alight.

The lamp shone over Noor's hard, sinewy body. She was a phantom halved in shadow and fire. One foot in this world, another in the next, moored between the divide.

Noor had been in this chapel before. Insomuch that every step she took was an echo from the past, her breathing quickened as the memories of the place flooded back to her. She remembered her slow march down the hallway, the weight of the coffin on her back, the scent of death and lavender wafting in the air. A procession of Fedayeen carried the bodies of their fallen brothers and sisters into the chapel; the dead were cloaked in white, immaculate shrouds and adorned with obsidian stones in place of eyes. Noor had watched the men and women burn in the pyre, the fire rising, taking back the fleeting spark of life.

She had been fighting wars for a long time now and they all ended the same. Blackened bones in a pyre. Meat for the faith's war machine. Nothing but grief and pain.

Noor's long journey had come to the end of the road. She was back where she had started. The showdown with her beloved would soon be over. Her day of reckoning had come. But now, on the verge of the closing act of her killing spree, she was afraid to see it all come to a close. What would she become when the night turned and her enemies were dead? Once this was all over, without righteous purpose, would she be able to stop killing?

She would never admit it out loud, but she had deep misgivings about the grisly path she was on. Deep inside her, she knew that something was wrong. These killings weren't sating her thirst for vengeance. Even after all this bloodshed, she felt no peace, only a growing need for more violence. She could've turned back and walked a different path from this one, but she didn't, and regrets were of no use to the damned. This cycle of revenge that she had chosen only took her round and around, lost, drifting, and going in endless circles, a self-perpetuating loop of violence that was spiraling out of her control.

Noor had to justify this slaughter, somehow. There had to be something more than the thrill of the kill or she would just turn into a monster. But she knew the truth about herself. Noor had no other skill but killing. Her hands were made for it. If she was going to settle scores, it would be on her terms, the only way she knew how, a rampage of violence, even if she had to sacrifice herself to do it. This had always been a suicide mission.

Steps tiptoed in and Kamal slipped inside the prayer hall. He was cowled in his black tagelmust and decked in a loose shirt of chainmail, his rifle gripped across his chest.

The Beiji's eyes looked spooked and as big as saucers.

"The janissaries are ready."

"Good," Noor croaked in reply.

Kamal covered his ears to the sounds of another explosion.

"The men look frightened," he said, maybe speaking more about himself than the mullahs' elite soldiers.

"Only fools feel no fear." She ran her slender fingers through the lamp's flame.

"We're going to war against a god," Kamal said. "Aren't you afraid?"

"There are no gods."

He approached, his voice low. "You've seen the creature. What does it look like?"

Noor grinned. She closed in and whispered into his ear, "She's big, hard, and battle armored. Teeth like razors. Eyes made of stone. There's no mistaking the Night Mother."

The kid swallowed and forgot to breathe.

"I'm joking," Noor cackled. "She is...beautiful."

The kid puffed up his scrawny chest, pumped the forestock of his rifle, playing up an affectation of manliness that didn't suit him at all.

"Your stories don't scare me," he sneered, but there was no bite behind his words.

"Let me teach you one last lesson," she said. "Don't be scared, kid; be terrified. Only terror will keep you alive long enough to kill your enemies and get your revenge."

"This rifle will keep me alive." The kid gripped the gun.

"All we have are the weapons in our hands. Nothing else matters in this world."

"What about keeping your promises?" he asked. "Paying back what you owe?"

"I have not forgotten what I owe, kid. When this is all over, I will settle scores."

Kamal backed off, and nodded, grudgingly.

Noor licked the nibs of her thumb and index finger and snuffed out the oil lamp with a waft of smoke. The light faded away, leaving them in silence and total darkness.

CHAPTER TWENTY

THE HERALD

Smoke billowed from the fires tearing through the remains of the great Kasbah of Samarak. The walls crumbled onto the streets, its towers collapsed into piles of broken bricks, mortar, and melted rebar. Screams echoed from the soldiers trapped underneath.

Kicking up a scatter of ashes, the Night Mother pulled the reins of her mare, stopping at the foot of an upturned wooden cross looming over the ruins of the structure. The young soldier chained to the beams outstretched his bleeding hand to her; his back was whipped and flayed clean of skin, the bones of his ribs glistened under the wounds. The black circle tattoo of a convert to the cult of the Black Dawn was inked between his eyes.

"What have they done to you, my child?" she asked, taking his hand.

"Mother..." the soldier's voice faded, the rattle of death behind it. "The mullah's armies broke through the Kasbah. Our men are dead. General Amin has fallen. It's over. The Fedayeen left me behind as a warning; they said I was the herald of their revenge."

"Don't fear, my child, I have a herald of my own." The dying star rose overhead and shadowed over the ruins of the Kasbah. "The Black Dawn. When that star reaches the summit of the horizon, its core will finally

come apart, unleashing all of its power to me. The mullahs have won a battle, but have already lost the war; they just don't know it yet."

"The revelation," he muttered. "It's finally come."

"My sons will rise from their graves. With them at my side, no one will stop me."

"Please," he begged. "I want to see it. The paradise you promised me!"

The Night Mother pushed back the folds of her robes, exposing her pistols and the hilt of a sword. "You can choose your gateway to paradise, my child. Bullets or the blade."

"I've never seen you draw that sword."

"Then marvel." She let loose the obsidian sword from its scabbard with a screech.

He began to cry, his upturned body shaking with laughter. "I see something..."

"Not yet," she said.

The Night Mother raised her weapon as a crack of lightning lit up in the sky and struck her obsidian blade; she aimed the sword on her soldier and launched a black fireball, burning the cross into a rippling blaze that spread across the Kasbah's ruins.

She approached her mare, who was spooked by the fire, and spanked its hinds to send it galloping back to the desert. The walk ahead to the star fire temple was something she must do herself. One last pilgrimage. A moment of silence before the world ended.

The Night Mother smiled as a star collapsed in the sky for her alone.

CHAPTER TWENTY ONE

SUICIDE MISSION

Noor took cover behind the Kasbah gate and zoomed her scope on the checkpoint of enemy soldiers patrolling the road. A barricade cordoned off the entire street, manned by ten soldiers and one falak reptile mounted with a machine gun on its hump. She turned to Cain and the detachment of janissaries crouched behind her. She shook her head, grimly.

"Trouble. Enemy soldiers and a war reptile are blocking the road to the temple."

Seth Cain snatched her night vision scope and scanned the check point himself.

"I don't like our odds," he said. "The machine gun on that reptile will mow us to pieces. I don't want to turn these soldiers into martyrs. What's your plan, Malatesta?"

"Easy," Noor snarled. "I'll draw their fire. Then we kill them all."

"That's your answer for everything." Kamal sounded nervous, crawling on his belly and adjusting the telescopic sights of his rifle. He looked shaken; the bodies everywhere had him second-guessing his own obsession with violence. He was a smart boy.

"Don't go soft on me, kid," she teased, noticing his hesitation.

Seth Cain unsheathed his saber. "This is suicide."

"Always was." Noor grinned, bolting out from the Kasbah gates.

Machine gunfire strafed the blacktop as she moved through the street, zigging and zagging her way closer to the checkpoint. The gunners emptied their cannons, burping smoke and cashed shells from the reptile's hump. Noor scudded across the road, bolted over the barricade, and drove her saber into a soldier's belly, lifting his body as a shield from the incoming bullets. Behind her, Cain and his unit swarmed on the check point, returning fire. The Fedayeen ignited his scimitar and slashed three men to the ground.

The enemy troops tried to rally together, back away, and retreat from their position, but they got caught in the kid's sights, and he picked them off one by one with his rifle. Noor chucked the dead soldier she was using as a shield and took her chances with the live crossfire. She lunged straight at the enormous falak coiled in the middle of the road. The gunners manning the machine gun aimed the weapon and strafed down at her. Noor landed on the reptile, lobbing a pair of grenades at them; the cannon detonated and fried the men with the blast. The falak bellowed as the machine gun burned, snaking away down the road.

The dying star rose overhead. Noor and the surviving men gathered around the dead; only Cain, Kamal, and two janissaries had managed to make it through the fire-fight.

Cain closed his scimitar on Noor. "I warned you this was suicide."

"Only death pays for justice in this tomb world." She pushed his weapon away with her own; black on red flames surged as the blades sparked apart. "I don't make the rules."

Noor wandered down the road, her boots crunching on rubble. The rest followed. She rounded the next street corner, entered an abandoned, open-air bazaar and raised her scope on the ziggurat looming over the city—the Star Fire Temple of the Eternal Red Sun.

Out of the corner of her eye, Noor spotted headlights gleaming from the road. A screeching gunship careened towards her. The cataphract revved its thrusters, jumped the curb, and roared into the arcade, shooting a round of bullets in her direction. Noor hit the ground rolling as the bullets zipped past her head. A cloud of gunpowder thickened the air all around her. Noor wandered through the haze. She scanned the bazaar with her scope, and discovered a body on the ground – the kid was down, gasping in a puddle of blood.

Noor scrabbled off the concrete and ran to his side. A surge of panic burned through her. She cradled his head in her arms and undid his tagelmust. He took ragged breaths and coughed red spittle. She held on to him, pressed her palms on the bullet holes drilled into his chest. The kid looked scared. He was cold and shaking and bleeding out fast. The Beiji's hands gripped his rifle, but were too weak to work the weapon. His fingers fumbled and slipped off the forestock. Kamal closed in on Noor, opened his lips, but no words came out. Tears streamed down his copper skin. Kamal was too weak to say it, but Noor knew what the kid wanted; the same thing she did, the only thing that gave her purpose, kept her heart pumping, and her body going—revenge. Noor took his hands, placed them on the rifle and lowered her chin on the muzzle. She couldn't stop trembling, afraid to die after all.

"Do it, kid," she winked. "A deal's a deal."

Kamal smiled softly as the rifle slipped from his grip.

Noor let go of the body and screamed in rage, all of her veins splayed and darkened. She snarled like a cornered animal, gnashed her teeth, and leveled her scimitar on the gunship. The rider piloting the cataphract circled closer, cannons smoking and overheated.

"I told you, you should've stayed dead," Sadira Rah said.

"And miss out on the fun?" Noor shook her head. "I don't think so."

Sadira Rah took off her helmet. A braid of jet-black hair dropped down her back from the base of her Mohawk. She glared at Noor. Dark veins crawled across her wild eyes.

"You will never save her," Sadira Rah cautioned. "Khadija is gone."

"It's too late for all of us. All we can do is burn." She ignited her saber.

Sadira Rah nodded, donned her battle helm, and sped the gunship towards Noor.

CHAPTER TWENTY TWO

THE FALLEN

The gunship accelerated across the arcade to mow Noor down. She held her saber in a forward, defiant guard, daring Sadira Rah to come and get her. Noor let the Fallen Fedayeen close the distance between them and ducked just as Sadira Rah's scimitar swept over her bald head, then slashed her own blade, gutting the cataphract's wing and fuel tank.

Smoke billowed from its side as the ship ignited, spun out of control, and crashed. Noor approached the wreckage cautiously, and watched the Fallen jump out of the flames. Sadira Rah landed in front of her, armor dented and scorched, while her blade raged on fire. The two Fallen Fedayeen walked in circles, pointing their scimitars at each other. Silence drew out until both women launched mirroring blasts of black flames across the arcade. The fire balls crashed and exploded, knocking them backwards with the detonation wave.

Noor struggled back on her feet, weak-kneed and fevered, and moved in on Sadira, who was already waiting for her in the center of the arcade. Close quartered, a few feet from actually touching, both women readied themselves for an intimate blade fight. Noor levelled her fiery scimitar over her forearm as Sadira Rah imitated her movements. The points of their blades teased each other and fed their growing flames. Screaming, they made their move. Quick, sudden strikes. Noor gored at the Fallen's head, but Sadira sidestepped the thrust, and plunged her own saber into Noor's ribs, splattering blood on the ground.

Sadira stalked around Noor. She always had been the stronger warrior, the better blade in the night, a Fedayeen blessed with a real connection with the stars, even dead ones.

"You reek of death," Sadira Rah growled under her battle helm.

Noor nodded. "I smell it too."

"What a waste..." Sadira Rah said as she speared another unexpected strike, slicing a gash into Noor's cheekbone. "There's no honor in killing a wounded animal."

"This always was a suicide mission for me."

The Fallen blessed Noor in the rites of their old religion. "Let me indulge you."

Sadira Rah slashed her scimitar in a relentless barrage, swinging right, left, and then back again. Noor struggled desperately to keep up and deflect the Fallen's assault, but the furious strikes caught her off balance, pushing her backwards against a broken column. Cornered like some low animal, Noor gnashed her teeth while holding her enemy's blade under tension. Suddenly, Sadira screeched the scimitars apart, and swung the edge at Noor. Noor jumped, skipping the blade as it struck the column and scattered a scree of marble. Screaming reverbed across the arcade as Noor swooped back down on the

Fallen with her fire sword, slicing through her helmet and chitinous armor, body cleaved into two smoking halves. The fire on Sadira Rah's scimitar went out as she split apart and hit the ground with a wet splat. Noor stood over her fallen enemy. Her blade sizzled and popped with blood.

Noor put out her scimitar as regret sank in; not for the blood on her hands, but for the end of her long journey, the revenge that gave her purpose and kept her going. Smoke lifted from the bodies around her and made the carnage become real and come alive. A cold sweat drenched her bald head. Her fever spiked. Noor needed sleep, more drugs, and maybe a coffin. But her cravings would have to wait. She had a friend to mourn and a lover to kill.

CHAPTER TWENTY THREE

THE NIGHT'S EYES

Noor walked around the bonfire burning in the middle of the arcade, her face blacked out under her ragged burnouse, repeating the familiar words of the prayers for the dead. Kamal lay at the foot of the pyre. He was naked, his copper skin freshly scrubbed with sand and washed clean with starshine, his eyes cracked with the effect of shattered glass. Noor knelt by his side and binded him in tight, fitted shrouds that covered his entire body. She cradled her pair of obsidian stones in her palm and then flipped the orbs into the air, but found no truths from the same-sided coins once they came back down. She placed the Night's Eyes over the kid's own to show him the way to other side. She had lit his funeral pyre, according to custom, in the middle of the arcade because the spot was open to the sky, a place where starlight would guide him to the fires that binded the galaxy.

Guilt gnawed at Noor. She had done the Beiji wrong, grifted him, and broken her promise to him. She owed the kid her life, but lured him out here to give up his own instead. She lowered Kamal's body into the pyre and watched the Beiji burn. Her eyes watered, streaking the ashes from her cheeks. She reached into the pyre and held the kid's hand for as long as she could stand the searing heat of the fire. But one pain didn't faze the other. It never did. All she had left was walking the tightrope between grief and madness.

"Goodbye," she sighed, licking at her burned palm.

* * *

The funeral pyre snuffed out in a waft of smoke as the petrol, kindling, and bed of wood died out. Kamal's body was reduced to gray ash, a skull, and the two obsidian stones. Noor dove her hand into the ash and held the obsidian in her fist, branding the hot stones into her flesh, and then put them back into the skull. The scars would be a reminder of her debt. The two of them were out of balance. His spirit would never forgive her until she paid back the people of this world and himself everything that she owed them. Noor prayed to the kid for his forgiveness, even though she knew she didn't deserve it. There was no other way out now. Her only choices were absolution or to die trying. Noor wasn't the woman she should've been, the hero this world needed, but she would become its instrument of reckoning. Her sacrifices had to count for something. Kamal wouldn't die in vain.

Seth Cain plodded towards her from the asphalt road. The Fedayeen took off his helm and blessed himself by the remains of the pyre. He lowered his head and prayed.

He placed his hand on Noor's shoulder. "He's at peace now."

"No." She tore away from him. "He is not. And until I repay him, he will never be."

Noor sat on an overturned column, hunched over, and sweating her infection. The gnarled wound on her ribs was throbbing and dripping blood down her new breastplate.

"Why do we burn the ones we love after they die?" she asked, sticking her fingers deep into the slit of her wound and rummaging the insides for pieces of splintered bones.

Cain sat next to her and took a long belt from his flask. "To cleanse their bodies from the sins of the world and light their path from the darkness of hell. Or so the story goes."

"Hell is the world," she snarled.

Blood bubbled from her wound as she plucked a sliver of bone. Noor eyeballed it, sniffed it up close, and then tossed the shard into the ashes of the pyre.

"We don't have much time," Cain's voice turned urgent. "The janissaries are all dead. Enemy soldiers are crawling around the temple. This is our last chance to turn back."

"There's no going back for me. I'm in too deep."

"Look at yourself." He smeared his gauntlet in her blood. "You're already dead."

"Maybe." Noor sparked her saber and cauterized the bleeding wound with the flat of the steel. She growled in agony. "But I'll drag the Night Mother to the other side with me."

"You're mad, Noor Malatesta," Cain said, "and you're going to get us killed."

"No doubt about it," Noor chuckled.

The Fedayeen crossed his arms over his broad chest and paced around the arcade. He looked out to the ziggurat towering over the blocks of scorched buildings around them.

"How do you plan on getting us into the Temple?"

"That's easy," Noor grinned. "We crash."

CHAPTER TWENTY FOUR

THE STAR FIRE TEMPLE

The cataphract sputtered a trail of smoke as it closed in on the massive ziggurat. Noor punched the accelerator and barreled the gunship through a blitz of artillery fire. Seth Cain hugged her waist as the shots raced past him, his hasty repairs had rendered the Fallen's cataphract airborne, but its leaking fuel tank was a ticking time bomb. Petrol already pooled near the thrusters and caught fire, threatening to blow them out of the sky.

"Hold on to your ass!" she said, narrowing her eyes into spiraling black-holes.

The gunship barrel-rolled past the salvos of anti-aircraft fire, crashed through the Star Fire Temple's stained glass dome, and crash-landed, skidding on the ground floor. Noor rose from the wreckage with her saber drawn. Cain followed her lead and panned his twin shooters, guarding their rear. She slunk around the hallway and took in the enormous statues towering all around her. The gunship had crashed in the middle of the hall of martyrs, a mausoleum of statues memorializing the Fedayeen conquerors of this planet.

"Let's get the action started," Noor croaked.

The doors to the hall of martyrs' slammed open and battle-armored Fallen burst inside, guns blasting. Noor and Cain took cover behind the statue of a squat, sandstone Fedayeen. A ricochet of bullets scattered across the great hall as the shootout intensified.

"They've got us pinned!" Seth Cain cried, sweeping his guns to return fire.

"No. It's the other way around. They're right where I want them."

Noor smirked at the fat, lecherous statue; she put her weight on her shoulder and slowly pushed against the effigy, teetering it back and forth. Seth Cain joined in, tackled the legs, and pushed until the top-heavy sculpture broke at the knees and went down, smashing headfirst into the firing squad, scattering the Fallen Fedayeen like flies. Cain raised his pistols and emptied the magazines in a roundabout, spraying a wave of bullets in a one-hundred-and-eighty degree turn, mowing the enemy stragglers running for their lives.

Black veins striped Noor's head, her body primed for another lowdown killing spree. She raised her weapon and hurled into the fight. Noor twisted her blade through the air and crunched into an enemy's helmet. Spinning, she slashed her saber in a low sweep, gutting the fighters coming at her from the flanks. Noor gunned it for the doors where a single warrior waited for her, blocking her path. The Fallen locked her in his rifle's sights. Noor rolled her eyes. She wasn't that easy a kill. Noor moved quickly, leveled her scimitar, and shot a black fireball at the warrior, charring his body to a skeleton crisp. She stepped over the carcass and moved out into the heart of the temple. Keeping her body low, Noor slunk through the halls and made her way to the upper floors, boots crunching on the rubble strewn on the ground. Her heart raced as she closed in on the stairwell to the summit of the Star Fire Temple. She stopped herself at the foot of the steps. A shadow bled over the tiles. Cain sidled to her side; his blade ignited for action. He studied the stairs, shaking his head.

"Something doesn't feel right, Malatesta," he said.

"It's a trap." Noor nodded, climbing up the steps. "Time to spring it."

The staircase ended at the temple summit, a glass paned cupula towering over the streets below. Noor crept up the stairs with caution; her scimitar in one hand and a blinking frag grenade in the other. Lights flared from the ongoing battle across the city and haloed the dark irises of her eyes. Suddenly, there was movement. Something shifted and buzzed up ahead. The shadow swept over the ground and then disappeared into the darkness. A low, wet hissing trailed behind it with an echo. Noor gnashed her teeth and backtracked.

"Not again..." she snarled.

"What the hell is it?" Cain asked.

"Scarab!"

Noor raised her saber and the Fedayeen followed her lead. The giant bug came into view, slowly, teasing its spindly legs, crawling out from an unlit corner of the cupula. Its carapace rocked from side to side with a chitinous sheen. The scarab splayed its wings, screamed, and barreled at them. Noor roared back at the bug. She swung her blade as the insect buzzed past her, cutting a horizontal gash across its carapace. The impact of the steel on its shell knocked her against a window pane, her bald head left a spider web crack on the glass. The scarab flew through the air and rammed into Cain, snapping its maws into his armor, and tossing him like a stone down the stairwell. Its mandibles wet and dripping, the scarab flew in a U-turn and scudded towards Noor. Noor pulled the pin off her grenade and lobbed it at the scarab. An explosion detonated across the cupula, but the scarab just went through the blaze and barreled at her. The bug bit Noor's hip, chewed into her, and broke through the window to the surrounding terrace. Noor crashed on the floor and rolled to the edge of the great ziggurat. Shards of glass bloodied her face with red, dripping war paint.

A bonfire rose from the solar pyre on top of the Temple. Black flames surged into the sky. The darkness radiating from the beacon called out to her. Noor steadied herself on all fours, crawling to the foot of the ancient altar. The solar pyre was the hearth of the Star Fire Temple; it was kept alive with the energy of Nahl Gul's sun. Noor's eyes went wide as the dark flames danced before her. She reached out into the beacon, touched a lick of the forbidden fire, and let a roiling inferno sweep over her entire body. Painful radiation boiled through Noor's veins. Her eyes rolled to black as she binded with the dead star and burned.

CHAPTER TWENTY FIVE

BLACK DAWN

That last red sunrise over the sky was a recurring memory Noor could never shake. A lick of the morning dawn baked her skin on the terrace of the Fedayeen Star Fire Temple that day, making her feel alive for the first time in a very long while. But nothing good ever lasted. Dread shuddered over her as the Mother's shadow swept across the temple summit.

The creature circled the solar beacon's ring of magnetic shields, the grid sizzled and popped at the touch of fire. She shot the shields with her pistols and watched the unrestrained flames rise to a towering inferno. Khadija's blonde curls and her defiant gait remained her own, but something disturbing lurked behind her blank eyes—a presence, altogether alien and merciless. She dropped a meteor rock into the bonfire and spoke an unknown tongue that made it crack open like an egg. Strange radiation spread from the meteor and flipped the flames from red to a ghostly black, exploding in a blaze of energy—a blinding beam rocketed through the air, breaking through the atmosphere, and shot out into space, hurtling faster than any ship in the Drus armada to strike the surface of the sun.

The star roiled with solar flares and almost went nova in the sky. But soon its fires started to flicker out; its surface banded with black scars as it was consumed by the darkness and slowly shriveled up to a charred, mineral core. After-burn radiated from the star's remains as the Black Dawn rose over the horizon and cast its shadow over the world.

The rebel Fedayeen, who had renounced their religion for the Mother's cult, stood in formation behind her, including the old members of Noor's unit: Sadira Rah, Sistani Amin, Joh Mustafa, and Reza Pasha; the warriors dropped to their knees as they were swept over and consumed by the pyre's flames. Noor's body burned in the fire with them. Her hair melted with the heat. Every vein in her body darkened. She doubled over with pain, but sensed something like pleasure hid behind it, her senses turning sharp and heightened. She had never felt this strong. Raw power surged through her as she binded with the dying star. She rose from the fire with the rest of her unit, unburned, blade alight with the dark flames.

Noor turned to the Black Dawn feeding off the light of the stars. Waves of guilt washed over her. She was having second thoughts about the path she was on, but couldn't stop the events already in motion. Noor and her unit had followed the creature into the temple and caught the Fedayeen by surprise, slaughtering the faithful who refused to join her. She'd reveled in a rampage. Enjoyed it, even. This wasn't who she wished to become.

On the temple summit, the Mother looked out on her dark creation and cackled. The shrill laughter snapped Noor out of her trance from binding to the dying star; she shook off the fear, gripped her scimitar, and lunged like a mad woman at the ancient creature. The steel drove into the alien's back, breaking through her armor and cracking into the bone. The Night Mother screamed and knocked Noor to the ground with a powerful deck to the jaw. Noor struggled upright, levelled her weapon, and backed up to the lip of the balcony. All around her, the Fallen Fedayeen closed in on her with guns raised and started blasting.

Noor jumped into the shootout, swung her saber, and cut Sistani Amin down with a slash, but the second round of gunfire stopped her cold and broke her dead in her tracks. Bullets drilled into Noor's chest and swung her around in a tailspin, pushing her over the edge of the ziggurat to drop down to the streets. She lost consciousness as she fell. Starlight filtered through the bullet holes drilled into her from collarbone to belly. A sharp pain woke her up when she landed. She cried out, spitting out blood. Sewage bubbled around her inside the gutters were she had landed. She worked on instinct alone and took in big, aching breaths, puffing up her shattered ribcage, and squeezed out of her armor. She tore her kameez and banded rags around the bullets holes drilled into her by the Fallen Fedayeen. Noor clawed the rusted drains, climbed out of the gutters, and struggled back on the road.

* * *

Noor came back to on the temple summit again, burnouse scorched and smoking. Her eyes blinked open and locked on the face of Khadija looming over her. Panic hit and her sweaty, radiation-fried body shook as she tried to backtrack from the creature. Her beloved was decked in mourning robes, trussed up under a layer of black veils. Khadija looked beautiful and tragic, her voiced was tinged with sadness, the echo a mother's grief.

The Night Mother reached out, touching Noor's cheek, "I've been waiting..."

CHAPTER TWENTY SIX

THE NIGHT MOTHER

The creature's reflection mirrored off Noor's steel as she backed away to the lip of the terrace. Everything went around in circles. Her life was a revolving cycle of death and fire. The saber tightened in her grip, sweat beading from her bald head to her chin. Cold fear pulsed through her, meeting the gaze of a flawless mirage of the woman she loved.

"If you mean to stop me," the Night Mother said, "you're too late."

Noor cackled, the sound of a blast in the background. "Seems a waste not to try."

The Mother lifted her mourning veils. "Fortune binds us together. One of us was always destined to kill the other. But, unfortunately for you, no mortal can slay a god."

Suddenly, a high-pitched screech echoed behind her. Noor turned on her heel, freezing when she spotted the scarab barreling straight at her. The bug's mandibles stretched out, dripping mucus and gobs of bile. She threw herself into the scarab's path, up-ticked her saber, and drove it through the insect's soft underbelly, splitting its shell into two, wriggling halves. Noor flicked a spatter of blood and offal from her steel and grinned.

"Is that all an immortal can throw at me?" Noor asked. "I'm disappointed."

The Night Mother drew her nickel-plated pistols and broke hell loose, firing a round of slugs across the temple summit. Noor jumped into the live fire, taking the bullets head on. One slug splintered the bone of her shoulder plate, the other two drilled into her chest. She swung her saber on the landing and struck away the creature's pistols to the city below.

"I can feel your struggle deep inside me." The Night Mother drop-kicked Noor ass-backwards to the ground with a boot to the gut. "The Black Dawn, it calls out to you, and draws you closer into its orbit, nourishes you with its power, making you stronger, faster, and far more dangerous. Accept your fate, take your rightful place by your mother's side."

"No." Noor spat a broken tooth. "All I got left is one last kill."

"So be it..." She peeled her obsidian war blade from its sheath. "This world doesn't belong to you. The paradise of the night and everything the darkness touches is mine!"

The Night Mother brought down the blade as Noor tried to block the devastating strike, but the Fallen Fedayeen's scimitar shattered to pieces like broken glass in her hands. Noor writhed on the ground. She felt the full brunt of the impact in every one of her bones. Her grip tensed on the remains of her weapon, a stiletto-thin shank attached to the hilt.

The walking mirage of Noor's beloved tiptoed closer to her. Khadija's bedroom eyes and playful smile were illusions of bygone and better days, but the poppy hallucination lifted the moment she stared into the creature's blank eyes. This wasn't the woman Noor remembered. There was no love left in her gaze. Only terror and violence.

A boom of thunder rattled the sky. Noor looked over her shoulder and watched the dark star overhead dim as its core faded out and a roiling storm of ghostly energy spread across the sky. Lightning descended on the temple summit like a plague from the legends of the end of days, frying the entire terrace with the blast from the corpse of the sun. The flames inside the solar beacon danced higher and higher, feeding off its strange energy.

Dark energy coiling around her, the Night Mother levitated off the ground and rose above the solar beacon. The creature turned to Noor as a crack of lighting split the skyline.

"Repent," her voice cut through the air like shattered ice. "The Black Dawn rises! And my brave sons return with it. The gates of the paradise of the night have flung open."

"You've gone mad!" Noor barked from the terrace below.

The alien creature approximated a grin. "Madness is unescapable for a god."

"It's the end of days," she said. "None of us are playing with a full deck anymore."

"Don't you see?" The Night Mother's stolen face lit up with the escalating lighting storm. "You and I walk the same path. One of us was always destined to kill the other."

Noor nodded. "Only death pays for justice in this tomb world."

She ignited her broken scimitar, flipped the shank like a propeller, and leapt into the sky, kicking up a wheel of fire, but the creature's sword was waiting for her. The Mother impaled Noor through the guts, skewering her body into the air. Noor tried to scream, but no sound came out, only bubbling blood. She glared at the alien across the length of the blade, dueling gun-slingers meeting over a narrowing battlefield. Aiming her shank dead-ahead, she pushed herself forward, swallowing the terrible pain down the length of the sword and plunged her shank into the Night Mother's eye and out of the back of her skull.

Dark flames rose into the sky as the women dropped into the solar beacon. Only the old lovers' shadows, bonded together in each other's arms, were visible through the seductive dance of the fire—their embrace disguised killing with an illusion of tenderness.

CHAPTER TWENTY SEVEN

THE RED DAWN

Darkness lifted as Noor pushed through the smoke wafting from the embers of the solar beacon. She was unburned; the skin of her legs, midriff, and bare back showed no sign of fire damage. Even the spider web of black veins stamped on her head was gone. Her eyes adjusted to the light and fixed on the slow burn of the red sun blossoming in the sky.

Noor balanced on the lip of the temple summit. A puddle of blood trailed behind her, dripping from her gut. She teetered back and forth on the ledge and looked down at the drop to the streets, cackling like a crazy woman. Noor clutched the war blade running through her, pulled the shaft out of her innards, and tossed the alien weapon over the edge.

Noor slipped in and out consciousness. She was running a fever and losing blood fast. Her eyes were closing. She was dying on this ledge, flipping the coin over to the other side, and she thought she was ready for it. This seemed as good a time as any to die. Noor was ready to pay back everything she owed. *Only death pays for justice in this tomb world.* She gazed over the budding red dawn shining over the city ruins and took in the scarred skyline: her only gift to this world. She hid it deep and hid it well, but her guilt had destroyed her. She was a broken woman, hollowed out, another ghost lost in the desert.

As Noor slipped away into a dark, dreamless sleep, she saw a vision of Kamal burning inside a funeral pyre. Her body burned with him. She reached out to him across the fire and held his hand tight, whispering to him, "Don't be afraid. I'm here. A deal's a deal."

The wind currents picked up. Noor's boots rocked backed and forth on the ledge. She opened her eyes, knowing that if she closed them again it would be for the last time. Noor wanted to do this right. She willed herself to keep going. Death was a one-time deal. She ignited her broken scimitar and cauterized her wounds shut to buy herself some time. Her eyes widened as she realized the red color of the flames; in the absence of the dark star, she was drawing her binding powers from a live sun. Maybe her hair would grow back too.

She turned from the edge and tracked her bloody footprints back to the solar beacon. Khadija's skeleton smoldered in a heap of ashes. Noor picked up her beloved's skull; the scalp was cracked open with the heat. Noor streaked a band of ash across her bald head like war paint, stuffed the skull in her robes, and disappeared back into the temple.

* * *

Noor waded through smoke rising from the fires burning inside the temple. She wandered through the corridors, trying to remember what this placed was like back when it used to be her home, but her memories had faded. Trying to bring them back brought her nothing but the sting of loneliness and pain. The walls of the temple were pockmarked and burned, the ceiling peeled back to the open sky, and the ground was cratered with blast-holes. Along the way, she picked up a collection of mementos from her old life strewn across the ruins, prayer beads, holy oil, ammo, and a rifle the same make as her old one.

Noor shook her bald head in sadness and looked around the ruins of the temple. This was the way of the world. This was how everything ended, in fucking pieces, with ash and dust. Her eyes slitted on a sputtering light on the other side of the hallway. She hedged for a split second but her curiosity only grew. A cloud of dirt whipped up behind her as she closed in. A large, unexploded warhead was lodged into a heap of concrete and mortar. Noor circled over the missile and gave the tip of the payload a sharp kick. Blinking, red bulbs lit up across the camber of the shell and began to rollback a precipitous countdown. The familiar thrill of running away from the scene of a crime rushed through Noor's entire body as she vaulted over the activated bomb and gunned it down the steps of the temple.

* * *

Out on the street, gunships reared over Noor's head, rocket fire detonating in the distance. Bonfires lit up the high-rises like torches. The stink of gunpowder, burning rubber, and the dead spread everywhere, wafting over the city like a widow's nest of veils.

Soldiers ran in squadrons through the streets, patrolling the main roads to the Star Fire Temple, speeding on armored cruisers and gunned rigs, clearing the surrounding buildings and alleyways, taking the best sniper positions over the rooftops. Standing on the opposite street corner, surrounded by a cordon of armed janissaries, a wounded Seth Cain, Maalik Raj, and the mullahs themselves were huddled together with their war generals. They spotted her presence from across the road and waved her through the security detail.

Noor jumped over the head of an overturned statue of the caliph on the intersection, and joined them. The janissary units trained their weapons on Noor, surrounding her as she approached the mullahs sitting under an expensive, tiger hide tent. Her eyes lingered on the young soldiers. Their bodies were braced, their blood was up, and they were ready for more action. She wanted nothing more than to indulge them, but playtime would have to wait.

"I would butcher every last one of you motherfuckers for a smoke," Noor croaked.

Seth Cain nodded to the janissary at his right. The young soldier saluted; he expertly rolled a cigarillo with his slender fingers and pink tongue, offering it butt-first to Noor. Noor took the cigarillo with her teeth and snapped her fingers until the janissary lit the cherry; she patted his ass softly as he stepped back into formation with the rest of his squadron. She took in a hit and coughed it back out almost instantly, face twisted in disgust.

"This is straight tobacco!" she snarled. "Don't you have any decent poppy?"

The soldier shrugged his shoulders as the rest of the janissaries sniggered.

Seth Cain limped over with his creaking, bionic prosthetic, the jet-on-red tattoos inked on his black skin highlighted by the waning artillery fire overhead.

"The last of the dark Fedayeen are dead," he said. "The creature's armies have been encircled or destroyed. Our forces have taken back the temple. No quarter shown or given."

"Sounds like a good time," she said. "Sorry I missed it."

Maalik Raj, the blind master of the Fedayeen Order, probed the ground with his cane and walked across the ring of armed soldiers. He placed his hand on Noor's shoulder.

"What about the Night Mother?" he asked. "What happened inside that temple?"

Noor revealed the cracked skull in her robes. "She's dead."

Maalik Raj blessed himself. "The mullahs' prophecies have come true. The devil is dead. The Red Dawn rises over the world again. This war is over. We have won!" The old man bowed at the three, fat little men sitting under the tiger-hide awning. "You have fulfilled your promises to me and redeemed yourself in the sight of the faithful. There is no reason for you to remain a stranger from the stars' fire any longer. The divine mullahs have agreed to lift your excommunication, forgive your many war crimes, and raise you to the ranks of the Fedayeen Order once more. You are to be shown mercy, Noor Malatesta."

"Mercy?" She pulled away from him and shook her head like she didn't understand the meaning of the word; her eyes glared over the grand master, brimming with suspicion.

"All you have to do is ask for it."

"What if I don't need your forgiveness?" Noor said, softly.

"You would reject the mullah's goodwill offer of mercy?" The old man's knuckles turned white on his cane. "Careful... Think well on your next step. It may be your last."

"I didn't go on this rampage to win a war for three little old men," she snarled. "And I didn't break free from your chains only to return to them willingly. If you want me, master, come and get me."

"My poor, child." Maalik Raj drew a blade from his cane. "Then you will burn."

"We all leave this world the same way we found it: a pile of bones."

Noor drew her scimitar one more time, hit the striker, trained her weapon on the three fat, little mullahs and burned the old men in a rage. The great mullahs of Nahl Gul incinerated into neat piles of ash and cooked bones. Noor grinned. There was nothing like the thrill of a hard fight, a close call, or a nasty kill; there was no harder edge than violence.

Maalik Raj swung his blade and crashed it against Noor's broken weapon, the flames dancing on the steel merged into a single, rising blaze, feeding off each other. Her old master pushed his weight on the blades, driving Noor back against the burning tent. She was pinned between one inferno and another. Space receded around her. Maalik Raj was a powerful, elegant swordsman, but no match for a lowdown killer fighting dirty. In a blur of movement, she kicked up her new carbine rifle and blasted Maalik Raj's head clean off.

Boots stomped on the pavement as the Fedayeen master dropped to his knees, smoke billowing from where his head used to be. The janissaries surrounded Noor, rifles raised, their lasers aimed, pockmarking every inch of her body. Noor blew them a kiss, flipping her fiery steel into a defiant guard. Cain elbowed his way through the soldiers.

"What have you done?" the Fedayeen asked, in disbelief of the carnage around him.

"There was only one way this war could end; with both sides dead and even."

"You've just signed your own death sentence." Cain drew his saber and flamed up.

"I did that the moment I started this killing spree." Noor eyed the janissaries, warily. "Now, tell your soldiers to back off. Don't make me scorch every single one of them."

"Stand down!" Seth Cain barked and the janissaries pulled back. "Let her go."

"Don't get any ideas about shooting me in the back, boys." She winked at the ring of soldiers aiming their rifles at her. "Nobody knows a killer's instincts better than me..."

"We'll meet again soon," the Fedayeen called out to her. "Trust me."

"No," Noor croaked. "We won't." Her voice faded with the boom of a large explosion ripping through the belly of the Star Fire Temple. The unexploded missile detonated. The blast blotted out the lights from the artillery guns as it rained down a fire storm on the ruins of the capitol. The explosion's after burn gleamed at Noor's back as she disappeared through the back alleys, leaving only a trail of boot prints behind on the road.

CHAPTER TWENTY EIGHT

PARADISE OF THE NIGHT

A lone cataphract sped through the outback and suddenly came to a stop next to a tar pit. Noor jumped ship and circled the dark pool. Bones of the outback's apex predators were half buried all across the desert valley around her. Ribs, horns, and saber-toothed skulls rose from the ground like the ruins of a skeleton city built out of animal and human remains. Scavenger beetles picked on the leftover gristle of a carcass beached on the pit. The skeleton bobbed aimlessly on the oily surface, scales sloughed off with decomposition.

The tar pits of the Bone Desert were known for their ancient reptilian graveyards; generation after generation of giant reptiles made their last journey on this earth to this place and ended their lives in their ancestral burial ground. The millennia-old ritual traced back to the prehistoric days before aliens or bugs or Drus walked the outback of this planet. The Bone Desert was the largest of the great deserts of Nahl Gul, but it was mostly uninhabited. Its pale hamada was a dangerous wasteland where beasts still ruled the wilderness and only mad men, desperados, and circus freaks dared approach. Noor hadn't decided which one of the three fit her best, but she was leaning heavy on the side of crazy.

Noor wandered around the bones strewn across the predator's graveyard in a poppy-fueled daze, surrounded by thousands of carcasses of reptiles, hyenas, tigers, and the other deadly predators that prowled the Bone Desert. She chomped down on a freshly lit cigarillo and pulled. The cherry scattered a shower of blue sparks with the wind. In the distance, her drugged out eyes saw a herd of reptiles moving across the horizon, but it was just a mirage, another poppy-induced hallucination. Noor was teetering on the edge of an overdose again; she'd spent most of her life sedated, testing the limits of her endurance, searching for a high that would mask the terrible emptiness she felt inside of her. She'd never discovered the trick to feeling whole again; this was one of her many failures. This was Noor's last chance at meeting her fate with a clear mind and eyes wide open. She tossed the cigarillo away.

She put herself to work, cutting down every tree and utility post she could find. On a low hill overlooking the valley, Noor stacked the logs into a tall pyramid and doused it in petrol and kerosene. With a grin on her face, she sparked her saber and set the funeral pyre alight. Self-immolation was an ancient Drus tradition; the rite had its origins in the stories of the Fedayeen warriors that fought the crusades of conquest for the caliphate. War prisoners and soldiers left behind enemy lines built suicide pyres to burn themselves alive.

Noor pulled Khadija's skull from her robes and stroked its smooth dome. They had never been apart for so long before; not since they first met at the steps of the great temple. Noor and Khadija were inseparable. They sparred together, worked in the same unit, and shared a hot, carnal bed. But, now, at the end, Noor could barely remember her soft voice. Soon enough, the lovers would find each other again, one last time on the other side; they had the kind of love that crossed the boundaries between this world and the next, but they were still lowdown killers, wicked women with an enormous body count, and they were both bound for one place: hell. It was where they belonged, their own paradise of the night.

Noor always knew it would end like this. Her killing spree had been fun while it lasted, but the show was over. It was time to move on and take the next, necessary step. Only death paid for justice in this tomb world and that meant Noor had to settle her debts. She owed this world a sacrifice, payback for all of the lives her rampage had taken, the friends she had disappointed, and the darkness she had helped unleash into this world. Noor had gotten her revenge, but this tomb world demanded its own. She'd thought the death of her enemies would bring her peace, but it didn't. The fire inside of her still burned. If Noor kept going, she would kill again and again, spiraling into another cycle of violence. Noor would never stop; she was out of control. This rampage had left her bloody, alone, and waiting for some hero to come and put an end to her. But no hero was coming, none were left to finish the job, it was just her out here. If anybody was going to stop this endless violence once and for all it would be herself, walking into a pyre like the Fedayeen of old.

The Red Dawn rose from the east, lighting the spine of the mountains surrounding the valley. Noor turned to face the young sun. A lick of the light warmed up her body and spiked her blood with a surge of adrenaline. It was at the end of her journey that she truly felt alive. Noor dropped to her knees and did something she hadn't done in a long while. She prayed, reciting the words of the prayer for the dead, cradling the skull in her arms.

She planted a wet kiss on the skull's dome. "See you on the other side."

With each step, Noor walked away from the rising Red Dawn, a phantom balancing the divide between darkness and the light, as she disappeared into the bonfire and burned.

www.ingramcontent.com/pod-product-compliance
Lightning Source LLC
Chambersburg PA
CBHW050900180626
46814CB00007B/2804

* 9 7 8 1 9 4 0 2 3 3 3 2 1 *